3am and Wide Awake

A collection of

thrillers and horror stories

From

Sarah England

Printed in the United Kingdom

First Printing, 2013 Alfie Dog Limited

The author can be found at:
http://www.sarahengland.yolasite.com

Cover image: Zacarias Pereira da Mata

ISBN 978-0-9569659-1-2

Published by
Alfie Dog Limited
Schilde Lodge, Tholthorpe,
North Yorkshire, YO61 1SN
Tel: 01347 827178

DEDICATION

For my dear friend, Debbie Dawe-Lane.

CONTENTS

Sarah England

ACKNOWLEDGMENTS

I would like to thank the following for originally publishing many of the short stories in this collection: My Weekly, Woman's Weekly, The Weekly News, That's Life Fast Fiction (Australia), Park Publications, Ether Books and Bridge House Publishing.

Thank you also, to Rosemary Kind, for all her help in compiling this anthology, and formatting it into a paperback version. I am hugely grateful.

1

3AM AND WIDE AWAKE

From somewhere inside the house a door slammed. And suddenly he was wide-awake, eyes straining against a wall of blackness, heart racing. He tried to call out but no sound came from his constricted throat, and his wife slept on. Tick-tick-tick-tick…Nothing there but the bedside clock…and …something else…breathing. Not his own. Someone there. Coming closer. He tried to move but his leaden limbs were paralysed. Watching, waiting, as out of the darkness a shape formed. Climbed onto his chest. Heavy. He couldn't breathe. He was going to die and he couldn't even scream. Then came the voice, delivered mockingly, "Good morning, Jack. Wakey, wakey…it's 3am."

***

9am

The medical receptionist looked up from her desk and gave the pretty, young drug rep a wintry smile. "Don't keep him long this morning - he's got a full clinic waiting."

Hayley Peters returned the glacial lip twitch and knocked on Dr McGowan's door. He was a nice guy, one of the few who offered her coffee and bothered to ask how she was keeping. Some of her other psychiatrist clients could learn a thing or two about that.

But today there was no cheery call to come on in. She knocked again. Silence. Well how odd! Cautiously Hayley pressed down the door handle and nudged open the door. "Hello?"

Jack McGowan's office was a modern box piled high with books and reading material, a testament to his volume of work. He had his back to her, staring at the computer screen. A blank computer screen.

"Dr McGowan?"

Jack turned with a puzzled expression, raked his hair and rubbed his face repeatedly, then gestured to the chair opposite. "Aaaah, sorry Hayley - bad night."

"The children?"

He looked shocking - grey pallor, red, peephole eyes - weary beyond all reason. Hayley hesitated, unsure of how to proceed. Perhaps a change of subject? "Feels like spring might be round the corner, still a bit chilly out, though," she said, reaching into her briefcase for a sales brochure.

Eventually he said, "No, It's not the kids."

"Oh? A difficult patient?"

"Sort of. Well, originally..." He tailed off, distracted, rubbing his face over and over as if deciding something. Then suddenly he poured out the story in a torrent. Something Hayley wished later, with all her heart, that he hadn't.

"It was Linda," he said. "We'll call her Linda - just out of prison and suffering from severe depression. She'd roll up in a ball in the corner of the ward and not do a thing you asked her. Just be looking back at you wild eyed, kicking and spitting if you went near. We tried everything, Hayley. Then I had this idea - hypnosis."

He paused.

Hayley waited.

"Shouldn't have."

Hayley looked around at the photos on his desk of a happy family life, of freckle-faced kids grinning at the camera, at his array of certificates on the wall, and felt an unaccountable stab of fear. This father, this doctor, this bastion of the established adult world, was broken. And about to tell her why.

***

Jack's Story

It had been a tough decision. Linda had been in prison for many years following an armed robbery resulting in the death of a security officer. Disruptive and tormented, she had finally been sectioned, since when she had become significantly more agitated.

"I want to try hypnosis," Jack told his colleagues at the team meeting. And soon after the first session, Linda had shown a remarkable improvement. However, less than an hour into her second session her demeanour suddenly changed. Gone the angst ridden young woman and in her place a grinning mask of pure malice. She began to speak in a deep, male voice, that called itself the Prince and began to make serious threats against Jack and his staff if they continued with this line of treatment.

To everyone's horror the Prince seemed to know every intimate detail about Jack's private life and that of his wife. Quickly realising that the demon was feeding off his energy, Jack tried to calm the situation down by meditating, and after a while the energy began to dissipate and the lights flickered. Linda became Linda again and the mask melted away. When she woke she had no recollection of what had happened and shortly afterwards, contentedly sipping tea, announced that she wanted to stop taking drugs.

But that night as Jack lay in bed turning over the day's events, the marital bed began to tremble and shake, gently at first, then quite violently. His wife remained sleeping. Jack, alarmed, switched on the lamp and the bed stilled. *Bad dream*. He glanced at the clock. It was 3am.

The following morning, shortly after he arrived at work a phone call from an angry colleague was put through. "Now look here, McGowan - I'm telling you now I have no intention of carrying out this ridiculous request. Quite frankly I'm amazed you had the gall to ask."

Puzzled, Jack asked him what he was talking about - he had made no request. The other doctor insisted it had been Jack who had left the message on his personal answer phone and would not repeat it for fear of embarrassing them both further.

Confused and not a little upset, Jack continued with his work before attending a lunchtime meeting. When he arrived at the meeting, however, he found his place had been cancelled earlier that morning and was refused admittance. The cancellation had been made by himself.

There were other oddities. His computer would flash up without warning, the printer would print unfathomable messages, lights dimmed and brightened and a book flew off the shelf. Then he'd picked up the phone to a caller who spoke only gibberish, except it was very clearly enunciated gibberish as if Jack should be able to understand. When he didn't the caller became extremely agitated and Jack had to put the phone down.

That night he lay awake trying to work out what was happening. Either he was losing his mind or some external force was influencing him. His wife, exhausted after her long day with the children, murmured something in her sleep and Jack sighed. He couldn't burden her with this.

Alone in the dark, his scientific mind tried to analyse the situation. But every avenue he took led him to the same conclusion: Linda's demon. He didn't want to believe it but what else could it be unless he was going insane? The demon must be inside him instead of Linda. She was better. He, however, was being tortured.

A crash downstairs and his eyes snapped open from an exhausted sleep. The night air sat black and heavy, a suffocating blanket. Something there. Edging nearer. A weight pressing down on his chest and hot, fetid breath in his ear, its voice silky and content, "You are mine now, doctor, and just think what I can do with your patients…oh what delicious fun I'm going to have…"

Jack tried to move his head away but found he could not. His heart was galloping, sweat pouring in rivulets down his forehead, dripping into his eyes, down his neck, soaking the pillow.

"We are one now, Jack. My perfect soul mate - so difficult finding the right host - evil and rotten. So important to have an…affinity…"

He wanted to scream, 'Never, never,' but no sound came. And his wife slept on. Downstairs the clock chimed. It was 3am.

***

He began to dread the nights. The big, comfy marital bed no longer the delicious sanctuary he had come to cherish.

"You look knackered," said his wife over breakfast. "We should book a holiday, Jack."

He nodded, distracted. Everything was normal. The kids were running round arguing and getting ready for school, the baby was whimpering and refusing to eat his boiled egg, the post plopped onto the mat and the radio played a familiar pop tune - '*So you had a bad day...*'

"What about the Canary Islands?" His wife was spooning egg yolk into the mouth of their youngest child - an apple-cheeked toddler with red hair and fat fingers.

"Yes, fine, book it. Oh, let me check the diary first."

"Do it today then Jack, and I'll get it sorted. Blimey, you look rough."

That night he slept downstairs, afraid to drop off, but inevitably he dozed, wrapped in the duvet from the spare room while the electric fire hummed and shadows played on the walls.

A loud explosion woke him.

On full alert, heart thumping somewhere in his throat, the first thing he noticed was that the fire was off and the room was cold. His breath steamed on the night air. Total silence.

"Who's there?"

He wandered into the hall to find the front door wide open and a stream of freezing air rushing past him. Closed it. Locked it. Immediately the study door slammed shut. Then the kitchen door. He stood alone in the hallway, waiting.

"Who's there?"

The darkness intensified. Tick-tick-tick-tick. A creaking door above him. He began to climb the stairs, overwhelmed with a feeling that something was very wrong up there. His children, his wife... Upstairs the darkness was thicker, almost palpable. There was a light on in the bedroom. His wife reading. Unusual but maybe she couldn't sleep, that's all it was. Nothing to be worried about.

He pushed open the bedroom door. But his wife was not in bed. And then he saw her. On the floor, her body cold and rigid.

After the initial shock, Jack grabbed a blanket from the bed and covered her. Her body was set to stone and icy cold and it took every ounce of his strength to drag her to the bed and then lift and roll her back in. And another hour before he felt her muscles gradually relax. Thankfully when she woke she remembered nothing except she 'didn't feel too good.'

Things were getting worse. He had to tell someone.

***

9.30am

Hayley listened with a mixture of disbelief and horror.

"Dr McGowan, you must get help."

Slowly he lifted his head. "Ah, Hayley, I know. I'm sorry. I shouldn't have burdened you, but…"

"It's ok, really."

He looked at her. "…I couldn't tell any of my colleagues or they'd have me committed!"

Hayley smiled. How she wanted to get out of here. "Glad I came in useful - I'll expect a lot of business after this, though."

***

But all day Jack's story didn't leave her and everything went wrong. '*So you had a bad day…*' Jack's secretary snapped at her for taking so much time. Her car wouldn't start. Her next appointment had been mysteriously cancelled and then she got a parking ticket. By the time she arrived home to find she'd lost her flat keys, she felt a cold coming on and looked forward to a bath and an early night.

She took a book to bed. The novel was a good one and, engrossed, she jumped at the sudden sound of breaking glass. Silence screamed in her ears as she strained to listen. Oh no - someone was inside her home, footsteps clomping down the corridor. This could not be happening. She caught sight of herself in the mirror - a blonde child-faced woman reading a book beneath a pink lamp - at the expression of fear on her face. Watched in horror as an elongated shadow of a hand crept across the wall behind her. And switched off the lamp. She tried to scream but no sound came.

Beside her the bedside clock glowed in the dark. It was 3am.

2
HEADACHE

I always believed that when we die, that's it. Finished. Kaput. The end of our tiny, inconsequential lives. Until I met Imelda.

Imelda was a temp at the office and I was one of the reps. We sold medical equipment - catheters and scopes - and occasionally I popped in to have a word with Guy, our sales manager. Only this particular morning, instead of Ruth, our regular Rottweiler in a twin-set, I was met by a willowy blonde in a mini-skirt. Not what you'd call pretty exactly - her dancing green eyes were a little too deeply set and her nose a tad too long for that, but she was certainly arresting.

"You must be Alice? Ruth's off today so I'm afraid you've got me." She held out her hand and smiled - dazzlingly unexpected. "You've got some new scopes over there," she said, pointing to a stack of heavy looking black cases. "There's one for each of you. Carol and Tina are coming in later."

Of course they were. Carol and Tina would have arranged that purposefully so they could have Guy to themselves. Vying for top jobs sharpens knives and Guy, being a straight kind of bloke, had simply told it like it was - that I was top in sales and first in line for his position when he gained promotion. Cue the end of two friendships and hello to professional isolation. I was unhappy, of course I was, and the unhappier I became the harder I worked and the harder I worked the more my shoulders, neck and head ached.

"Ooh, careful," said Imelda as I bent over to pick up my case, wincing with the pain that shot up my neck.

I smiled, the kind of smile you see on ballerinas faces when their shoes are too tight. I had some painkillers in the car and I didn't want to linger. I rarely stuck around for chats - running onto the next mission then the next, collapsing when I got home with a pounding headache. But Imelda seemed nice and it certainly made a change not to be glared at by Ruth or whispered about by the other girls.

"Don't worry," I said. "It's just stiffness from driving. I ought to see the doctor, but, you know…"

"Oh it's not that," she said. "You're carrying around your dead brother's spirit with you - that's what's doing it."

She stated this fact about as casually as if she'd said my shoes were rather nice, and I stared at her open mouthed. Well, it's not what you expect in everyday conversation, is it?

Imelda laughed - a real head-thrown-back, belly laugh. "Your face!"

I laughed too. Ooops. I'd been had. Too tired to spot a bit of a leg-pull.

"Come and have a cup of tea in the kitchen. I've just put the kettle on and Guy's out until lunchtime. We can get to know each other."

I hesitated.

But evidently she wasn't taking no for an answer. "I've got some aspirin in my desk. I'll go get them."

Well before I knew it she was telling me everything I kind of knew already but somehow didn't - that Carol and Tina regularly popped in to see Guy, always managing to tell him how uptight, stressed out and over-ambitious *I* was. They said I was running from business call to business call, working late into the night, didn't know how to relax and had *no people skills...*Imelda was on overdrive and I had to stop her.

"Sorry. It all sort of rushes out of me. The thing is, you're running away from yourself, from your own shadow..."

"I've always been like that."

"Alice - you need to speak to your mother and soon because this spirit is catching up with you. You can't run away forever. He's part of you. And he won't rest."

"Um...speak to my mother?" *About a brother I never had*? Was she crazy?

Imelda nodded. "So, didn't you know you had a brother, then?"

"I don't. I'm sorry, Imelda. I have two younger sisters and that's it."

Imelda looked back at me with a deeply unsettling gaze, and said. "But he's here, Alice, I can see him. He's called Frank. Ask your mother about him."

And then she was gone, leaving me in the empty kitchen with the blinds flapping and the fluorescent lights flickering overhead.

It shouldn't have but it did. The whole thing bugged me. So much so that when it got to the weekend I just had to bring it up with Mum. We were alone in the kitchen after Sunday lunch. She was washing and I was drying. I took a deep breath. "Mum, er, um, look I don't know how to say this but...did I ever have a brother....?"

My mother's response was to drop a plate. The crash shattered the air between us and I watched horrified as her bleeding fingers scrambled around amid shards of china still glistening with soapsuds. "How could you, Alice? For goodness sake."

"I'm sorry. It's just that this girl at work said I had a dead spirit hanging around me, and that he was causing my neck pain."

My mother glared at me through flinty eyes. "For neck pain, Alice, you see a doctor."

So I saw a doctor. In fact, during the following weeks I saw a physiotherapist, a masseuse, a chiropractor, an acupuncturist and an osteopath. But the pain racked up and was worsening by the day. Soon I could barely leave my flat without taking a cocktail of painkillers. Yet the pain increased until I could barely see. And maybe it was my imagination, but as my temples throbbed and an imaginary axe sunk into my cranium, I could have sworn my shadow was becoming longer. And darker.

People began to back away when I spoke. Focusing on something slightly beyond me instead of on my eyes. And when I lay in bed at night, my fuddled brain played tricks on me - black shapes sliding around the walls and heavy breathing in my ears. I'd sit bolt upright, panting, afraid. Someone was in the room.

"I think you need anti-depressants," said the doctor. "And I'll refer you for a cat-scan."

So he thought it was a brain tumour, did he? I wondered what he'd say to the theory of it being a long-deceased brother I never had? Nobody believes in stuff like that. Everyone would say I was crackers, losing the plot, having a breakdown, as ga-ga as Lady Gaga. I think at that point I began to lose all hope of ever being cured. I could just imagine the gloating when Carol and Tina heard I'd been signed off for stress and depression …

"Two months off!" Imelda gasped on the other end of the phone.

"I know. But what can I do? I can barely function."

"Frank's getting angrier, Alice. He doesn't like it that his own mother denied his existence."

"Imelda - I can't ask her again. She was livid."

"You must. Or, how can I put this? If you don't you will *never* be well."

Her words were like a punch to the gut. Nausea clogged in my throat as my shaking fingers ended the call. This could not be happening. Okay, so Imelda had some kind of psychic powers, I could accept that. After all - just because we can't see something it doesn't mean it doesn't exist. But this whole thing was sorely testing my rational mind. There was really only one thing I could do at that point, I thought, and that was to disprove it.

On the drive over to my mother's the pain was blinding and I had to pull over several times. I took the maximum amount of analgesics advisable and drove with blurred vision.

"You look awful." said my mother, opening the door.

"So do you."

"Had a few sleepless nights. Nightmares." As she stood back to let me in, she rubbed her eyes repeatedly, and I noticed how utterly drained she looked - grey skin tone, unwashed hair.

I followed her into the kitchen and waited while she put the kettle on and spooned coffee into two mugs. She plonked the hot drinks on the table and we sat facing each other through coils of steam.

"Mum?"

She winced. Knew what was coming.

"Mum, you have to tell me. Just answer me. Please. Did I ever have a brother?"

She glared at me. Then, slowly, her lips began to tremble and her eyes filled with tears. Finally she nodded. "You had a twin. He was born just minutes after you but..." She stopped and I reached over to take her hand while the impact of what she was telling me sunk in. "There was something not right - he was very tiny. He didn't survive more than a couple of hours. We called him Frank."

Frank!

Immediately she caught the look on my face and pulled back. "I'm sorry, Alice. I know I should have told you, but there never seemed to be a right time and in the end poor Frank was just one of those things we had to put behind us."

The previously sunny kitchen flickered into darkness and we both gasped. Imelda's words echoed in my head: *Frank is angry - he can't understand why you're denying him.*

"Mum - Imelda says we have to acknowledge him. It's the only way."

"Alice - who on earth is this woman?"

After I described her, Mum shuddered and said, "She sounds a lot like the Imelda I knew as a little girl - your gran's sister. She died of polio when I was in my teens, though. How odd."

We talked and talked and as we did the atmosphere lightened and gradually I became aware of the pain inside my head lifting. We parted on happier terms than we had in months and as I headed out to my car an hour later, I realised something - my neck and head pain had completely gone.

At first I couldn't quite believe it. I danced around, doing a little jig. Imelda had been right. All we had to do was acknowledge poor little Frank. Because here I was - free of pain at last.

The next morning I rang the office to tell Imelda the good news. In fact, I planned to take her out for a meal - anywhere she wanted.

Ruth answered. "Imelda who?" she snapped. "Never heard of her."

"Imelda. You know, the temp while you were off? Blonde hair, mini skirt?"

"I haven't been off."

"But she made me tea in the kitchen…" My words trailed away as understanding crept in. Imelda had appeared at my side out of nowhere that day, and since then I'd only ever spoken to her on the phone. My skin chilled as if I'd stepped inside a tomb.

Only Ruth's voice, shrieking out of the handset, brought me out of my shocked silence. "…so did you want something then?"

I'd been going to say I was coming back to work but found myself saying something else entirely. I told Ruth I was handing in my notice. Risky, yes, but in my euphoria I was pretty sure I'd find a happier place in which to work. I could do anything - I was at the top of my game. I imagined Ruth's face - like the rear end of a turkey - and giggled.

Later, still thinking about Imelda, I sauntered out to the car park, swinging my briefcase in the sun, twirling my keys. Good-bye, Frank, my baby brother - gone to a higher place. Rest in peace, little one. No more headaches, no more running. No more long shadows. I twirled around - and then the smile died on my face.

The pain in my head was so sudden and so violent I crashed to the floor, vaguely aware of someone tall and blonde, walking calmly towards me through a fine mist as if she had all the time in the world. No mini-skirt this time though, just a long brown coat and a gentle smile. "Hello again, Alice."

Oh, I didn't meet an untimely end if that's what you're thinking. No. I woke up. I could hear them talking first of all, saying how if only I'd gone for the cat scan they would have known about the aneurysm. And then how odd it was that the ambulance arrived so quickly when there was no one there but me - unconscious and lying on the floor.

Gradually their woozy faces came into focus and I realised I was coming round from an anaesthetic. "You're going to be fine, Alice," someone said. "You must have a guardian angel."

I still see Imelda from time to time - today she was behind the bar at the local pub lecturing me about drinking too much white wine after work. Another time she'll be in a bus queue or passing on an escalator. A quick glance of flashing green eyes and an impish grin and my heart will jump. My guardian angel? A spirit who decided to stay on after the job was done? I don't know. But I do know this - I'm quite happy to wait a very long time to find out.

3

A SECOND OPINION

Two weeks after Marlene's cremation I found her sitting on the sofa. I'd just walked into the lounge and nearly dropped my tea.

"Oh for goodness sake, Geoffrey," said Julia, diving for the carpet with a wad of kitchen roll. "You're getting so clumsy in your old age."

I looked again at the sofa. That could not be Marlene. She couldn't be sitting right here in my house. It wasn't possible. And yet she was. I swear. As shockingly real to me then as she had ever been, smiling wanly as she faded into the upholstery.

"Well I expect it will come out eventually," Julia was saying. "I've still got some of that carpet cleaning stuff we…" She looked over at the sofa then back at me. "What? What is it?"

"Nothing. Trick of the light, I expect. Thought I saw something."

The woman I murdered.

It had been, I quickly reasoned, a stab of inconvenient morality. A memory, which in time would fade. *Get a grip old boy! It's done with.*

Yet my age-spotted hands shook badly as I lifted the teacup to my lips. And my heart jittered about in its increasingly brittle cage. What an old fool I'd been. One with an important career and an influential wife. But in the end - still a fool.

It was Saturday morning: papers, breakfast, and Radio 4. A low autumn sun bathed the room, dust motes twirling, settling on us an air of timeless golden contentment. Children grown and gone. All those years stretching ahead of us. Just as it should have been. And so nearly was.

Marlene, I thought, staring for so long at the same paragraph in The Guardian that it blurred...*This should have been over.*

***

We met during an angioplasty: a routine procedure that saw Marlene, the anaesthetist, switch from boredom to panic in less time than it took for me to nick a major artery. The man died and the case went to court.

We consoled each other over a few shots of single malt in her flat overlooking the river. Rushing, giggling water. Crisp, white sheets. Plunging oblivion...

On the day of her funeral three months later I had a full operating list, beginning with a quadruple bypass graft and not finishing until well after her coffin had been lowered into the furnace.

"You're sweating a bit today, Sir," said my Senior Reg.

Inside the latex gloves tiny globules of guilt rolled into the wrists. God it was hot that day. Hot as a furnace. With wobbling, clammy fingers it was damned near impossible to thread the sutures while visions bulleted through my head - of flames leaping gleefully into auburn curls; racing across alabaster skin that melted and popped. Cauterisation, I told myself, it was our own cauterising filling the air with the sickening stench of burning flesh, not...

"Are you all right, Sir?"

"Bit below par, Anderson. Might grab an early lunch."

The graft had been a success, but it was best I thought, to leave the rest of the list to him. Flu, I said. Something like that.

Half an hour later I was sitting outside the little pub by the canal we used to frequent. One day replayed inside my head: Marlene sitting with her face to the sun while I talked about a clinical paper and a trip to Tokyo to present it. Maybe she would like to come?

She'd smiled and reached across the table. "Oh Geoff, I've never been so happy. I feel like running barefoot through the grass, or wading up to my thighs in the river, or making love in the bluebells. I feel alive, Geoff."

Her voice was loud and people were looking. I pulled back my hands. "Right. Well, um, must get back to work - clinic this afternoon, old girl."

"Why don't we take a walk instead - see if we can find somewhere secluded?"

I hesitated. There she was - all bouncing, coppery hair, smiling up at me with those bewitching, feline eyes. The pictures she conjured of lying together in long, dewy grass while light-filled leaves danced and swayed above us, enchanted my days and taunted my nights. In the breath of a summer breeze came whispers, and in the cool caress of her fingertips, warnings; yet still I'd wandered down the dark path of iniquity, led by the hand into the forest like a fairy tale fool.

A life-time ago.

Julia, of course, fussed when I arrived home early. "Flu? Well you do look pale. You've been over-doing it, if you ask me…"

I didn't ask you.

Her voice peck, peck, pecked at my head. "...and you're getting on. Why don't you think about retiring, Geoffrey?" On the phone to her sister, "Only I'm worried about him...not even reading the paper... not concentrating. Of course he won't go the doctor. He is one. Knows everything..."

There were days I'd wake up and look at this woman, and wonder how I had ever fallen in love with her. Eons ago our stars had snuffed out and been replaced with the endless, grey dawn of a dreary reality.

With Marlene, though, the light had been blinding. We found every spare moment, every inappropriate place, every excuse. To say I'd dreamt, yearned and longed for her...no description came close to the hormonal, unthinking force that propelled the stranger inside to act as he did. Long after Julia had sunk into the soft oblivion of sleep, I'd lie starkly awake replaying every gasp, every touch, every throbbing pleasure in all its dizzying detail until I'd thrown off the covers, waiting for the fever to abate. Which it had to, of course. And did. Although not in a way I could ever have imagined.

It was the weekend of the August bank holiday when all three children came home with husbands, girlfriends, and toddlers. A heavy, airless day that sapped energy, blistered lawns and melted tarmac.

Marlene sent a text. She must see me and it was urgent.

Bloody selfish, I thought. She knew the family was here this weekend and now I had to sneak off like some kind of cad. Couldn't the woman spend just one day on her own?

She was waiting by the canal. Usual place.

"Geoffrey. I'm so sorry but I had to..."

I looked at my watch. "Marlene - I've got the whole family here."

A tiny muscle twitched in her jaw. "What about me?"

"Oh come on - you know I'm married."

It caught me unaware. Suddenly her face crumpled. She dipped her head and began to rustle around in her bag. Out came a syringe.

She caught my look and snapped, "Insulin."

"Oh… I didn't know."

"Hmm. Well my blood sugar's all over the place at the moment on account of my being pregnant."

Her mouth twisted into razor wire, the elfin face suddenly vixen. "I matter too you know, not just your wife."

'Wife' came out in a spit.

In an instant the fever dropped and my head cleared. Leaving a mind that began, with laser precision, to analyse the available options. All of them exacted a toll.

I took care, of course, to veil these thoughts, while offering the required words of comfort. And as she subsequently slept with cat-like satisfaction - stretching, nestling and murmuring - I saw the needful child, heard it fracturing the night with its screams, and snapped into decision.

A full vial of insulin sat on the bedside table. It wasn't difficult. A moment.

***

After her debut appearance that Saturday, Marlene's ghost followed me everywhere. During Monday's clinic I called for the next patient, looked up and there she was - seated on the consulting room couch.

A voice from far, far away, said, "Are you all right, Geoff?"

Still riveted to Marlene's image I barely heard the nurse.

"Do you want the next patient?"

Breathe, breathe…

Clinic seemed to run on interminably. The waddling, wheezing sick. Old. Smelly. Stupid. Or all of the above. Afterwards, I grabbed my coat, dashed across the darkening, rainy car-park, sparked up the ignition and stopped. Turned. Oh so slowly. She was there. Right next to me in the car. With bruises for eyes and dripping coils of blood-red hair. Such an enigmatic smile as I screamed and clutched at my pounding chest.

Go away, go away, go away…

Everywhere. She was everywhere. In the canteen queue. Lingering in an empty changing room. At the breakfast table next to Julia munching on cornflakes.

A month later I took annual leave.

Guilt. What else could it be? I took sedatives. I pottered in the garden. Ate healthily. This would fade in time. Of course it would. Yet lying in bed I knew that if I opened my eyes she'd be there - watching me while Julia turned the pages of her Margaret Atwood.

"Geoffrey, you're soaked," said Julia, peering over her bifocals.

I turned away. An old man. A frightened old man in sensible, striped pyjamas.

"You look grey. Is it angina?"

What did she know? I was the God-damned doctor and it wasn't that.　　Another week and I agreed to see Howard, a psychiatrist colleague. I was, by that time, pretty sure the visual hallucinations were symptoms of clinical depression.

Howard nodded while I talked. Depression was, he

agreed, a likely cause - the death of a lover, an encroaching retirement - it all made sense and as he confirmed my diagnosis, relief washed over me. It could be treated.

I returned home feeling more optimistic. After a hearty meal, I popped the first tablet and wandered into the bathroom, planning an early night. Only to find Marlene reclining in the bath. Corpse white. Lips the colour of crushed tomatoes, hair cascading like Ophelia. She smiled and held out her arms.

Another week and I was admitted to the psychiatric wing. The duty nurse took my blood pressure, clerking me in, when Marlene appeared at the end of the bed. I leapt back, gripping the sheets. Somebody was whimpering like a child.

Was that me? Was it? Was it me?

The nurse stared.

"Do you see anything? Tell me you see something!"

Somewhere a door slammed, the sound drifting down the corridors along with the schooldays aroma of beef and boiled vegetables.

"Perhaps," she said, "a sedative, Geoffrey?"

"Sir." I reminded her.

More tests were taken. "We'll run the whole gamut," said Howard. "Give you a thorough MOT, old chap. Physical and psychological. I'm sure all you need is a bit of peace and quiet but We'll check you out properly."

Behind Howard, Marlene sat playing with her hair, smiling to herself.

Breathe, breathe…

"Do you believe in the hereafter?" I asked him, as she merged with the painting on the wall into its sea of bobbing boats.

Howard regarded me, his mind working through the list of possible diagnoses just like I would have done myself. "It takes time for the treatment to work, Geoff. Let's give it time."

I shook my head. Psychotic symptoms flirted erratically with pure madness, and my brain was all I had. A first-class, brilliant mind turning to jelly. A story of pity - students standing round my bed watching me dribble and giggle in a backless hospital gown.

The guilt was festering, poisoning my mind and it had to be lanced: a wound would never heal while still infected. Howard would understand and then he could give me a properly informed second opinion, and I could be treated and go home. Invite him over for dinner.

Behind Howard, Marlene nodded. It was the only way.

And there was patient confidentiality. This rolled into my rationale. Along with the fact that psychiatrists never divulged their patients' secrets. Never. The medical profession protected each other. Look how Marlene and I had covered each other's backs when the GMC asked questions.

And so, on the gathering rush of an impulse, I released my guilt. How in the early blue dawn I had taken a needle and slid it beneath Marlene's creamy skin. The woman was going to blast my world apart.

Two days later Howard came to give me the results of the tests. I stared with mounting horror while he calmly and almost apologetically explained that macular degeneration had caused something called De Bonnet's syndrome, which can result in highly disturbing hallucinations. The good news, however, was that it could be treated successfully.

I need not have confessed. Just one more day and I need not have confessed. But worse - far, far worse - I should have known. Should have diagnosed myself for God's sake.

In the corner Marlene started to laugh quietly. Shortly after I began the course of treatment, however, she stopped laughing. Probably because I couldn't see her anymore. But then, I never saw my wife again either. Just four white walls and occasionally the prison warden's face peering through the grille in the door.

4

BURNED

It began and ended in a darkened room - blinds fluttering in a breeze scented with freshly mown grass, dust motes dancing in shafts of sunlight and the distant sound of children playing outside.

Slowly I opened my eyes, becoming aware of the hiss and hum of machines on either side of my head, the clattering of a trolley beyond my room door and a telephone ringing. Hospital then. I tried to move but couldn't. Oh sweet Lord. *I couldn't move.*

Calm down…deep breaths…this may not be so bad. But there was something in my throat. I looked down at needles piggy backed and taped onto the back of my hand, at the bruises, purple and black on the other one, as if someone had practised a few times and failed. *Something in my throat.* My head felt stuck to the pillow. I couldn't stand it a second longer. Couldn't breathe properly, *something in my throat…*

Next a loud beeper started to buzz. A door crashed open and people burst in.

"She's awake."

"Hello there, Emily. Can you hear me?"

So that was me then - Emily.

My eyes were streaming. I was gagging. "Good girl. Now breathe out and We'll have this tube out of your throat in no time, okay? One. Two. Three…"

"The interview," I croaked. I can't believe it now - that they were my first words. They looked at each other as if I was out of my mind. "What about the interview?"

A nurse leaned over, smiling kindly, and took my hand. "Now, now," she said. "All that can wait. First things first."

But I had to know. There I was, barely conscious of my own name yet needing to know before anything else if I'd got the job - the one I'd been working towards for years and years, my whole adult life. There was a mortgage. We were behind with it -a problem. Yes, and a credit card bill. We? Harry. Oh no. Harry!

People flurried around, filling in charts, wheeling away machines, asking 'Helena,' who I presumed was my nurse, if she would be okay. She said fine, checked my saline drip, adjusted it, then lifted my wrist with cool fingers while my life flashed in bullet points. I'd been running across a car park chattering into my mobile. The sky… Yes the sky had been a bizarre mix of floating soapsuds spiked with thunder grey. A strong wind buffeted the soapsuds, changing their shape from whipped ice cream to ghoulish, floating gargoyles. I was lying on the ground. Being lifted… Cold, so cold…

"Where's Mum?"

"She's here. We'll fetch her in a minute."

When my mother came in she was all bitten lips and darting eyes. Not what I'd expected. No rush of relief and shining gratitude. That was my first inkling that something was badly wrong. She needed reassurance. She couldn't look at me.

The words cost me, my throat as raw as if it had been sandpapered, my mouth dry. "How long have I been here?" I was thinking two days maybe three.

My mother sat on an orange plastic chair, stroking my hand, eyes focused firmly on the top of my head. "A few weeks."

Weeks? "How many?"

"Six."

Six. *Six weeks*?

The shock was like a jackhammer to my heart. Nausea clogged my throat and hot blood rushed to my head, blinding me. "So…why? Why have I been here all this time?"

"They had to keep you in a coma," she explained to the top of my right ear. "Because of the injuries, Emily. The burns. You've been in a car crash."

Yes, that made sense. Bits of it were coming back to me. So the worst was over then? On the mend now? Yes? I could go home soon and be with Harry. "Where's Harry?" I asked her. *Yes, by the way, where the hell was he?*

My mother stared at my right ear for several more heart thumping seconds before answering. "He, erm, came…but, look it might be best to wait a while, Emily."

Like mist slowly lifting off a murky swamp, soft puffballs of confusion floated away, leaving me with a sudden and stark comprehension: she'd said *burns.*

"Could I have some water?"

Nervous glances. Why did they keep doing that? Helena took over. "Let's prop you up a little, sweetheart." She leaned me forwards slightly to plump up the pillows, slotting in an extra one before expertly hoiking me up underneath my elbows as if I was feather light. "There we are."

The sensation was funny, as if the glass that should have touched my lips had actually been put straight inside my mouth. My head felt as heavy as a cannonball, my tongue swollen and huge. I glugged the water, coughed, gasped for more.

"Take it easy."

More nervous laughter.

"Okay," I said, leaning back, swallowing over and over. "How bad is it, then?"

My mother's terrified eyes locked on mine. She nodded, squeezed my bruised hand.

"That bad, huh?"

It was a month before anyone dared bring me a mirror.

***

The last thing I remember was walking towards my car. I was high, distracted. They'd loved me. "You're perfect," they said. Of course I was. I'd won every sales competition going. And when I smiled I had the face of an angel, or so I'd been told. Something of a distraction, Harry used to say. "That's why they buy from you - because they can't see anything else, not even reason. Like me."

It was a big step though, that interview. The biggest leap - from sales up to management. I could do it, of course, everything they asked of me and more. But I could see them looking at me too, like everyone did back then, thinking maybe I should be selling perfume instead of cardiovascular drugs.

Actually I quite enjoyed the way I looked: swishing my long, golden hair from side to side when I walked; smiling cheekily when I wanted someone to sign on the dotted line; flashing wide green eyes at good looking men when we passed in the street. It was fun. Easy. God-given.

The man interviewing me had been handsome,

shrewd; the woman hard-bitten. But she knew I hadn't had it easy. One glance at my CV told her that: an ordinary comprehensive education, night school to get the grades I needed for university, waitressing to pay my way, seven years of tough cold calling, working my way up through the company, passed over for promotion time and time again.

Such were my thoughts as I crossed the tarmac on that fresh spring afternoon, with the phone clamped to my ear talking to Harry. It was time. Oh sweet rewards. Those clouds, jostling and bouncing. I'd been smiling up at the heavens - feeling full of hope and joy even when the first few spatters of rain flicked against my cheeks - as I clicked off the phone and swung my car keys round and round my fingers. As I jumped in, crunched into reverse, foot down...

***

They brought in someone specially trained in things like this - a woman carrying an extremely tiny mirror. She said it was best to do it in stages. Had she been in marketing it would have been called a slow reveal - surely the most irritating form of presentation. So I grabbed the mirror and held it so I could see the whole lot.

I knew my skin would be burnt. But nothing could have prepared me for the face in the mirror. Criss-crossed with deep purple lacerations, my forehead was now the colour of an over-ripe strawberry, the hairline no longer where it used to be. I lifted the mirror up and up, tracing the reflection of my never ending forehead as it ate further and further into my scalp like a racing tide on wet sand, to finally end with a few bristly, burnt out tufts.

On some kind of sadistic quest I kept going,

swallowing rapidly, as the horror show unfolded.

"Do you want to carry on, Emily?"

I couldn't stop.

I thought back to all those furtive glances when my visitors thought I was nodding off, the enforced jollity of conversation and the initial flinch when they walked in the door and caught sight of me.

The skin across the central panel of my face was tight as if a red balloon had melted and stretched across it, distorting my nose to one side, pulling down one eye below the other. Moving the mirror down I saw that where there had once been full, peachy lips there now lay a gaping hole, which left my gums exposed. The hideous red mask spread further yet - down to my neck in great, beetroot coloured wrinkly splashes like someone went crazy with a paintbrush. And then stopped. Except for a couple of broken bones and fractured ribs that still had me pinned to the bed.

The funny thing was - I truly believed I would recover. That blinding human condition called hope. I was fine. It was just my face. A bit of make-up. A visit to the hairdresser's when my hair grew back…What - about a month before I could go back to work?

It wasn't until a week later when I was standing under cruel fluorescent lighting in the ward bathroom that the slow dawn of reality reached its destination and finally punched me full in the gut: m*y face was never going to get better.*

They brought back the lady with the mirror. "There's surgery you can have,' she said. "A specialist you can see."

I would have cried again - those great heaving, wracking uncontrollable sobs that had me crumpled on the bathroom floor, but it made my eyes sore and I knew by then that once I started I wouldn't be able to stop, and the more I cried the more it would sting my raw skin. Mutely I nodded.

***

Eighteen months later I was wheeled out. The finished product - ta da! They'd wrapped me in a blanket, put a scarf around my face and plonked a hat on top of my head. Penny for the guy. I breathed in the glorious damp, autumnal air - bonfires, fog, decaying leaves - and shivered. People pounded the grey pavements, bags knocked against me, passing cars thumped with music.

"Here she is," they said. "Our brave girl."

My room at home was just as I'd left it as a teenager nearly a decade before. A row of stuffed animals eyed me silently from the bookcase as I tentatively put my suitcase down on the pink rug in the pink room with the pink curtains - whatever phase I'd been going through had definitely been a girly one. Bare chests of grinning teenage boys, now men with histories of rehab and numerous children, leapt out at me from the walls. This was only for a few days. I would be going back to the house soon. When Harry came for me.

Harry had rung. Said sorry he hadn't been back to the hospital after that first visit. He couldn't deal with it, but now I was better could he come over? Perhaps he thought that like a broken doll I'd be magically fixed, I don't know, but I'd had all this surgery by then, wore a cute beret and special make-up, and I thought I looked okay. Not like before, granted, but I'd kind of got used to the new me.

Two days later I opened the door with my lop sided smile in place.

Harry stared, then lunged bravely to fleetingly kiss the side of my head. "How've you been?"

There was a time when he'd hug me a dozen times a day, couldn't, he said, believe how lucky he was. Now he perched beside me on the sofa like an estranged nephew with a maiden aunt.

"Great. Much better. The company rang - said I could start back at work if I'm up to it. Tea?"

"Thanks." He took a sip, trying not to watch mine dribble down the side of my chin. "The house is coming along great by the way."

"I'd like to see it."

His eyes betrayed him. "Yeah - course. Well as soon as you're... uh-hum... settled."

"I'm settled now."

I paid for half the deposit on that house, my salary still paid half the mortgage. But by then the feeling was familiar, of everything slipping away, secrets being kept - my life, my promotion, my fiancé, my house...'

"Right."

"Harry - I'm still me, you know - inside?"

He squeezed my hand without looking at me, and I knew then. Knew he couldn't do it.

After that my manager came to see me. Bouncing through the front door, he greeted my mother, booming about meeting me, where was I hiding, so happy she's out of hospital...He rounded the corner into the lounge where I'd been dozing. I'd forgotten my beret so he got the full picture, and almost leapt against the wall. "Ah!"

That night I cried. For the first time since being in the hospital bathroom I sobbed and sobbed, great convulsions that had me folded in a heap like a collapsing deckchair. Why had I worn a nylon polo neck sweater that day? A fibre that caught fire and burnt my face and hair in seconds. Why hadn't I seen the oil tanker changing lanes? The hot hatch right on my tail? Why, a thousand whys, and most of all - why me?

No answers came, only the straitjacket of an unavoidable truth: there was no way out. My life as I knew it, was over.

Welcome the soothing dark cover of night with its blindness and its kindly blanket of black velvet that sheltered me from a world full of horrified stares and prying questions. Oh they all wanted to know - what happened, oh you poor love, come away children, don't stare, oh dear me - have you seen?

Waiting for the grey fingers of dawn to poke through the curtains, it occurred to me that this was who I was now. Still me, still here, but with another shell.

All some time ago now, of course. A decade. Since then I graduated in fine art, and Harry married someone else then left her. The guy who got my promotion? Had a nervous breakdown.

Now I only lie awake briefly as dusk slips into night. There's a fleeting pain. And then it's gone.

5

MASQUERADE

The street party outside was setting her nerves on edge. Shouts too close to the windows - like a crazy, pitchfork wielding mob baying for blood. Gwen, who was going through the cupboards in the bedroom upstairs, paused. Listened. Someone was climbing the steps up to the front door.

"Go away," she muttered under her breath. "Just go away."

The rat-a-tat-tat fractured the silence, echoing sharply round the house, gloomy now with the curtains drawn against the murky darkness. Shadows lurked on the walls like unearthly watchers. A floorboard creaked. Gwen held her breath. *Go away.*

But the rat-a-tat-tat came again. Louder. Insistent. The fist of a man. Gwen looked at the cat lazing on the bed and the cat looked back at her, ears flattened, not pleased at the disturbance to its tightly coiled sleep. The darkness, so thick it was almost a physical presence, pressed around her as she strained to hear. Good: the footsteps were retreating. Could she risk a peep between the curtains? Or would one of the revellers notice? Too risky.

She stayed frozen, knees still bent from sorting through boxes and clothing, as she mentally worked through the security situation: the curtains were closed downstairs, doors bolted from the inside, windows shut, a couple of lamps on. Surely the intruder would infer that no one was home? Everyone at the party? But those footsteps hadn't finished. Clomp, clomp, clomp. A squeal of the un-oiled side gate. Clomp, clomp, clomp. Round to the back door. Bolted, yes, but only glass. Thud, thud, thud!!! One gloved punch and he could be through.

Picturing a blurry face behind the frosted panes, and an ominous dark shape inches away on the other side, Gwen's hands squeezed into white-knuckled claws, her heart pulsing hard in her throat, her neck. *Oh please, please - just go away.*

What made this person think everyone wanted to party, anyway? To sing and dance with painted faces and ghoulish costumes? Couldn't they leave people alone and let them make their own decisions? The event had certainly been publicised well enough - no one could possibly have missed all the posters and leaflets. There had been cards in the shop windows, banners strung from lampposts, and schoolchildren banging on doors selling tickets - it was tricky avoiding the little blighters! No, everyone would know about tonight's party in the park with its fireworks and loud music. And most were going.

"There were never things like this when I was a girl," she said softly to the cat, who stared at her as if she was out of her tree. "I blame America."

The cat yawned and stretched, kicked and wriggled a little, then curled up to resume where he left off - satisfied that the crisis was over.

Deeming it safe but just to make sure, she stood on creaky knees and edged towards the window to peer hesitantly round the edge of the curtain. With a start she jumped back - a warrior with a spear was plodding back up the driveway, leaving the side gate swinging open. Charming! Still - at least he was gone. Good.

A low mist had settled in, swirling around lanterns and torches like spectres in the night. Against the yellow fuzz of the streetlights, a fine spray of determined drizzle was dampening glittery costumes and banners, but not spirits. The mass of bodies swayed as one, moving like a giant centipede down the street towards the park opposite - lanterns dancing, pointy hats bobbing, children in fancy dress laughing and shouting, "Everybody out! Party, party, party!"

Gwen let the curtain swing back into place. They ought to know - not everyone wanted to party, thank you very much.

It hadn't always been this way. Once her home had been a beacon of family warmth - the thunder of tiny feet on the stairs, doors slamming with petulant, "It's not fair, but why can't I..." tantrums. Doors flung open on balmy summer evenings and always something tasty wafting from the kitchen for the boys after football practice. Sometimes, on winter evenings, George would light a real fire and they'd make toast over it with George's granny's old toasting fork. "We had to do this when I was a kid," he'd tell his wide-eyed sons.

"What - you mean you didn't have a toaster?"

"Nope. Nor a dishwasher, nor a microwave or even a colour television."

They started to laugh. "Dad - you're making all this up!" "He's just teasing, Tom - don't believe him."

"And we certainly didn't have air-con or heating," George went on, warming to his theme, "My mother used to put hot bricks in the bed in winter."

Gwen smiled sadly as she made a start on the dressing table drawers. They hadn't had much money, not on George's wages as a cab driver and her a full time mother, but they had laughed a lot - a close and happy family. And enjoyed simple pleasures like playing a game of Monopoly or sharing a homemade chocolate cake while they watched Saturday night television - good in those days, she remembered, lots to make you laugh. Not like today's obsession with crime and hospital traumas.

She worked swiftly. Clearing. Sorting the wheat from the chaff. The time had come, and it all boiled down to this - what could be sold? And goodness knew, she needed the money.

A tidal wave of rage threatened to engulf her yet again, making her head spin and her fingers fly faster. She shouldn't have to do this, especially not at her age. This should have been a golden time of reward, of holidays and grandchildren, a time she had looked forward to after years of washing underwear and sports kits, of scrubbing the grimy bathroom and picking up wet towels. Now this. Damn George, upping and leaving after all those years, taking his redundancy money and his fancy piece 'for a new life in America.' *Thanks George. Thanks a bunch!*

Maybe she'd brought up the boys a little too well? Alfie had graduated from university with a first class degree, which had opened up a top job for him in London. And Tom had disappeared - backpacking in the Far East, where he was now teaching English and planning to marry a local girl.

All of which left her here alone - rattling around in a house whose ceilings seemed to reach ever higher and whose rooms were expanding. A house she could no longer afford, kitchen drawers crammed with letters written in red ink, wallpaper peeling and rugs frayed. The boys would be appalled if they knew to what level their mother had sunk.

Nearly finished. Gwen sat back and gazed at herself in the dressing table mirror, ghostly in the lamplight: pockets of sadness under her eyes, pinched mouth - sucking lemons as George used to say - and a turkey wattle neck. She pinched the tissue skin over her voice box. It stayed in the pinched position - a tiny peak of crepe. So here she was - resorting to selling possessions in markets and on the internet, counting out small change so she had enough to eat. And now the house was going - repossession. *Thanks, George.*

Still, the dirty job was almost done. Gwen stood up.

The first firecracker made her jump as if a gun had gone off and she had to steady herself. Crack. Crack. Crack! The cat flew off the bed in a streak of fur. A cacophony of fireworks fizzed and a cheer went up. Then came the bumf, bumf, bumf of pounding music. Through the curtains she could see the bursts of colour exploding in the sky, and almost smell the smoke, sizzling hot-dogs and frying onions. Tears stung her eyes. Party time. Parents holding onto tiny, excited hands. Faces aglow as the fireworks flew, popped and sparkled, lighting up the black night in a brilliant blaze.

Get a grip, Gwen. Finish the job.

Quickly she placed everything saleable into a large rucksack and then padded quietly downstairs. In the kitchen she shrugged into her black hoodie and picked up her ghoulish party mask and torch. Then slid out of the back door and melted into the throng unnoticed.

A street party. Everybody out. A good night for cat burglars, and tonight there would be rich pickings.

6
ADELE

There she lies, skin white as alabaster, as perfect in death as she was in life.

'I'll leave you then - for a few minutes,' the mortuary assistant says in hushed tones, barely above a whisper.

The door shuts softly behind me. We are alone, Adele and I, with the humming emptiness of the morgue. Perhaps her spirit watches me from somewhere above my head, peeping over the water pipes, as I shuffle towards her still, statue like body. I wonder what she sees. All that warm pulsing passion, now swept cruelly away to leave a tear stained straggly haired youth in an ill-fitting suit, flailing around hopelessly without her. My beautiful Adele.

I bend to kiss her cool marble forehead. Unreal. See the curve of her immaculate eyebrows - like inverted ticks - the elegance of her long, feline eyes, and the soft fan of black lashes on sculpted cheeks. The fullness of her plump cushioned lips draws me towards them but no, wait. They will be cold. She is dead. Adele is dead. No more the crush of heated, pulsating skin. No more the heaving of her body against mine. Adele is dead, dead, dead.

I drop my head, feeling a cool draft of air against my

clammy skin, clearing my head, lifting the nausea. It wafts over the white sheet that covers her body from the neck down, rippling over the swell of her breasts down to the hollow of her stomach, clinging to bony hips and long, slender thighs. Would her toenails still be painted in the blackberry polish I varnished them with less than two nights before?

Sometimes they'd be blazing red, other times gothic black or candy pink. 'Paint them,' she'd say, flinging herself onto the sofa next to me in the middle of a football match, long, bronzed legs draped across my lap. 'Come on, Guy, you do it so well,' with a cat-like knowing smile. Of course, I couldn't resist. I never could, not from the first moment I set eyes on her.

Adele had been a model, whereas I, well, I suppose you could say I was ordinary - training to be a solicitor, mid-twenties, played football or rugby at weekends, drank in the local pub with a crowd I'd known since school. I was one of those people who never expected much to happen. I'd been seeing Dawn, who works in the bakery, for a few months but all that changed the night Adele walked into the pub. Pow! Imagine a comic character with his eyes popping out on alarm clock springs from his eyeballs. Imagine heart signs in neon pink pinging from his chest. Imagine all conversation ceasing. That was the Adele effect.

No one quite knew why she picked me, though.

She said she was a receptionist. At twenty-eight too old to be a photographic model anymore. 'Rubbish,' I told her, running my hot, eager hands down her naked back. 'You still put the rest of them in the shade.' She'd smiled and purred, incredibly, unbelievably, happy in my bed with me, in my two-bedroom terrace house.

There was one thing though. The gloves. 'I can still do hands,' she said, explaining their presence shortly after we first met. 'That's why I wear these. Don't ever make me take them off, okay? They've got to be milky white perfect or I don't get work.'

She always wore them - white cotton usually. Black satin in the evenings. They added a slightly old fashioned, lady-like touch to her glamorous image, like a latter day Audrey Hepburn or Princess Grace. I didn't mind. At first. It was one of her eccentricities.

I knew, of course, that she'd had her breasts enlarged. She openly admitted it. The lads down the pub called her Jordan. And of course she'd had her teeth done, no denying that when they flashed dazzling blue-white in between her pouty lips. It didn't matter. Adele was stunning. If she'd had a bit of enhancement, so what? She was a model; it was her line of work. And she was a beautiful woman - all mine. Or was. The real mystery, as people kept reminding me, was why on earth a woman like that had ever wanted to marry me.

'He must have money.' I heard the whispers. It insulted me. But worse, it insulted her. What we had, whether the gossips liked it or not, was love. It was me who wanted to marry her not the other way round. And me who tried to persuade her to model again. 'No more publicity, Guy,' she'd say, cuddling up beside me on the sofa. 'Just you and me, that's all I want.' She was content with me, you see, enjoyed me fussing around after her, running her baths, painting her nails…

I can still see her the day she moved in, surrounded by designer luggage, cat eyes flashing, long, blonde hair cascading down her back to skin pinching white jeans. Cote d'azure meets Rotherham. It was raining outside, spattering the window, dirty brown streets with people running to their cars. The image was surreal, haunting, and will stay with me forever.

In contrast to her everything in my house suddenly looked old and shabby. Adele wanted new. We'd have it, I told her. One day I'll be a corporate lawyer and you'll have everything. Oh how her eyes shined. All new. I'll buy you a mansion I said, a gothic palace. She liked that. Anything oddball, unusual, eccentric. It was one of the many things I loved about her - that what you think she was, she wasn't, that what you saw you didn't necessarily get. I loved everything about her. Except the gloves. I began to not like those. I wanted, begged, to feel the caress of her fingers on my skin, to see the glint of my ring on her finger.

She'd smiled enigmatically, touched my face with a cotton cool hand. I don't need a ring,' she said. 'Just you.'

That last night we'd danced, bodies brushing, lights down low. The next day she would have been my wife. Except she collapsed in my arms.

'Ah!' The door behind me swings open and I spin round to face a balding man holding a pile of notes in a file. He eyes me for too long a moment over heavily rimmed glasses, a slight knotting of the brows, while his voice echoes around the room, bouncing off tiles, piercing the gloom of my thoughts. 'You must be the son?'

I look at him askance.

'I take it you are the next of kin?' he asks.

'Son?' What son? There were no children. Besides, at six foot two I could hardly be mistaken for any pre-pubescent schoolboy. Of course, he has the wrong room, wrong patient, wrong body... Oh God. Bureaucratic incompetence. My voice is snappy, harsh. 'No - no children. I'm Adele's fiancé.'

Now his brows leap together to form a long black line. He checks his details again. 'Adele Watson, right?'

'Yes.'

'Born fifth September 1950?'

'No.' For goodness sake. 'She's twenty-nine.'

Confusion swirls, catching us in its chilly breeze. We stare at each other. I can feel my nostrils flaring. How can this idiot be so badly informed, so insensitive?

And then something in his expression changes and softens. 'Ah, I see.'

He gestures to a chair. I ignore him. There is a touch at my elbow. I shrug him off.

'She went suddenly, didn't she? I'm afraid her poor body couldn't take anymore.'

'Couldn't take what?' I'm thinking drugs now, secret drinking…Oh Lord, what hasn't she told me? 'They said she had a weak heart.'

'Well her heart couldn't take any more, that's for sure. Not after the last lot of liposuction. I take it you knew about that?'

I shake my head. I am vacant, empty headed - nothing makes sense.

He moves swiftly on. 'There was an infection. It seemed the antibiotics didn't work. They tried almost everything on the spectrum but nothing…She was taking painkillers like Smarties. '

'Liposuction? Painkillers?' Perhaps it was the honeymoon in the Caribbean? Adele, ever the perfectionist, must have wanted to look even better than she already did. Why oh why? She was perfect to me. My thoughts are racing, so much so I barely hear what he says next.

'You didn't know? Ah," he says again, clearing his throat rather awkwardly. 'Well, ah hem, she'd had rather a lot of surgery in the last few years.' And he begins to recite as if from a catalogue. '…a face-lift, a brow lift, a neck lift, dermabrasion, laser resurfacing, a breast augmentation. Twice. Underarms tucked, liposuction to the abdomen and thighs, cosmetic dentistry with full implants upper and lower. Ah yes, and Botox. It's all here. I'm afraid she must have been rather, er, frugal with the truth. She was fifty-seven.'

Swaying sickeningly, I clutch at the table she lies on.

'Look,' he says, lifting the sheet to take one of her delicate hands in his. It is crinkled like used tissue paper, crepey and blotched with light brown shapes. It is the hand of an old lady. The one part of herself she could do nothing about. 'Did you never look at her hands?'

It is only then that I let myself see the tiny, white scars tucked beneath the hairline of rich, golden hair, the telltale fine silvery threads that run deep beneath the golden tan, tracing along the inside of her arms and her tanned, toned belly. Only then that I see how fragile the image. And only then I realise what she had seen in me - and wanted so badly. My youth.

7

MOVING IN

The rat-a-tat-tat came late at night. Panicky. Urgent. Rosemary put down her paperback. The wind soughed in the trees outside and the fire crackled in the grate. Perhaps she'd imagined it. But then the knocking came again. Shaper and more insistent. *Let me in... let me in...*

With a heavy sigh, she prised her creaking joints from the comfy armchair by the fire and shuffled painfully into the flag-stoned hallway with Paddy, the Labrador pattering behind, to unlatch the heavy oak door.

In a whirl of spiralling leaves and freezing fog, the visitor stepped into the old house, hair falling in a dark, silken sheath as the hood of her cloak dropped back.

"I'm Alice," she said, holding out a slim, pale hand.

Rosemary's face creased into a frown of confusion.

"Your sister," explained the stranger. "You *are* Rosemary Fairfax?"

"Sister?" She needed to sit down. She had no sister. This woman had made a mistake. But it was a dreadful night, so..."You'd better come through. Here - let me take your coat."

Then over cups of reviving tea, with firelight dancing on the walls, Alice began tell her story like a wicked stepmother reading an evil fairytale to a gullible child.

Rosemary's eyes widened and her heart fluttered wildly in her chest. This was just a bad dream, surely? If only she hadn't answered the door.

"Only when my mother died there was nowhere for me to go. Just think - we must be about the same age, Rosemary!"

Alice's dark eyes danced with amusement. Both women were sixty-two, yet while Rosemary was clearly a make-do-and-mend sort of woman cushioned with plenty of cream cakes, Alice looked like a fashion editor.

"I'm so sorry," said Rosemary, avoiding the unpalatable comparison. "Did your mother die recently?"

Alice nodded and the room appeared to darken. Abruptly she stood up and began to wander round the room, picking things up. This is nice and that is nice. As if calculating the value. "Nice place..."

"Well..."

"...our family house," she added with an impish grin.

Our?

Rosemary's stomach plunged. Of course! If Alice was her father's illegitimate daughter from over sixty years ago then she was here to claim her half of the house. But where did that leave her? What ever would she do?

Pointedly, Alice looked at Rosemary's white knuckles gripping the chair.

"Actually, Rosemary, you make me rather sick," she said, putting down her teacup as calmly if she'd just said she loved the wallpaper.

"I beg your pardon?"

"Here you've lived your lovely life until you're handed the family house. You've never had to do a single day's work, have you, Rosemary?"

How far away from anywhere they were. With belts of thick sea mist rolling in over the fens, coiling wetly around the old house, stilling the trees and muffling animal cries in the night.

A tight little voice that Rosemary realised was her own, squeaked, "It's late.   Perhaps you ought to go. We can discuss this another time."

"Oh I don't think so." Alice sat down and poured herself another cup of tea.   "At first he'd stay with us from Monday to Thursday. No doubt your mother assumed he was at his club? Actually, sometimes he took my mother there." She smiled briefly. Before a thunderous cloud gathered behind her eyes and her voice hardened to flint. "But not often. No, you see usually, Rosemary, my mother would be sewing and sewing until her fingers bled. And in the evenings she'd sew some more for private clients - people like you - until her eyesight failed."

The smash of cup on saucer was sudden and violent, and a gasp echoed around the room as Rosemary's hands began to tremble and her teeth chattered like a child's.

"I'm sorry." she said.

"You're sorry!"

"I didn't know."

"Neither did I. I didn't know about spoilt little Rosemary while my mother was taking in washing. Didn't know about the big house when we had a back yard terrace with damp crawling up the walls. He left us, Rosemary. Of course I realise now that he was here all along with his comfortable country lifestyle and his fat little daughter ..."

"Stop!" Tears sprung into Rosemary's eyes. *Fat little daughter...*"What do you want from me?"

Alice sat back in her chair and gazed hypnotically into

the flames. Then after what seemed an interminable age, she said, "What I want, Rosemary, is a home. A place to stay."

Her words settled between them. "It's just that since Ma's gone there is nowhere, you see. For me."

"No."

"But now I've found you. My dear half-sister. I'm sure it's what our father would have wanted, aren't you?"

Nausea clogged in Rosemary's throat.

Alice stood up. "I'll leave you to think, Rosemary."

Rosemary's body seemed to crumple with relief. Alice was leaving. Going. With a bolted door behind her. Let the solicitor handle it now.

It was only after three fractured, sleepless nights that she decided to take matters into her own hands. Alice must be plotting her next move and any day now a white envelope would arrive courtesy of an expensive London solicitor. She had to act fast - find out who Alice and her mother really were. Such were her thoughts as the train trundled down to London.

Alice's mother, Ada, was easy to find, having died recently, and further searching produced the births register for 1947. Ada had a little girl called Alice on the 17th November, and there, scrawled in thick black ink for all the world to see was evidence of her own father's betrayal. So Alice was who she said she was. Goodness she needed a stiff drink. But there were no other children, and Ada had never married. How odd. Odder still that an attractive woman like Alice hadn't married either. Why? Why didn't she marry?

Perhaps the answer could be found where they'd lived in East London? She'd have to go there. All those years - someone must know something. Emerging from the tube station, Rosemary paused to question the wisdom of this decision as dust bunnies of litter scurried across the deserted streets. Tap-tap-tap with her stick. All alone. Silly old fool. Should have left it to the solicitor. Who did she think she was - Miss Marple?

Still, she was here now. Although she wished wholeheartedly she wasn't. Most of the terraces were boarded up and the one corner shop had grilles across the window. Ada's house, it transpired, was one of the few still lived in. But why would a smart, clearly successful woman like Alice want to live here too? And for so long? Perhaps her mother wouldn't move?

There was no answer when she knocked on the door. Maybe a neighbour would remember Ada? Anything. A clue to the truth, that was all.

Eventually a small, rotund Indian lady in a golden sari appeared at a window opposite and waved. Rosemary's legs were heavy now and feeling the strain.

Fortunately the lady was kind - putting the kettle on and calling a taxi to take her back to the main station. "No more tube for you," she said, shaking a ring-laden finger. "Not with those ankles."

Gratefully Rosemary sipped the fragrant tea as she explained why she'd come.

"Poor Mrs Ada. I miss her, you know? She was such a lonely, unhappy old lady."

"Lonely? But what about her daughter?"

Her host looked puzzled. "What daughter? She didn't have one."

"But she did. You see - Oh it's a long story, and the taxi will be here in a minute, but well - the daughter came to visit me and it seems we're erm, half-sisters. I think - you know, after the war…"

The lady's brow creased. "No," she insisted. "No daughter. Mrs Ada was so upset because the girl died of pneumonia at seventeen. Alice she called her. She never got over it and never married. Poor Mrs Ada. I used to do readings - kept her in touch with the other side. Oh look - my brother is here now with your taxi."

It took a while for Rosemary to fully comprehend what had happened. There would, after all, be no terrifying, crisp white letter falling on the mat. And no more late night visits. Paddy looked up from his basket while Rosemary prepared the evening meal, muttering to herself. "I'm just a silly old sausage," she chuckled. "Must have dreamt the whole thing."

And yet. The old house creaked so. A calm day and suddenly a door would slam, followed by the squeak, squeak, squeak of her father's old wheelchair working its way across an empty upstairs room. Tea-cups disappeared then re-appeared, and silvery voices whispered in corners.

Just the silly imaginings of an older woman living alone in a large house on the fens, you might conclude. A house full of dark furniture, heavy paintings and family secrets. A house which echoed to the tune of a turbulent past. That's all. Nothing more.

All the same, Rosemary decided to make up a bed for Alice in the garden room. After that, sometimes, when she tottered up the path with a bag of shopping or a trug full of garden vegetables, there would be a shadow at the window and the inescapable feeling of being watched. But no more trouble.

Alice must, at last, be content Rosemary decided. Now that she'd moved in.

8
DIFFERENT COLOURS

Funny how a throwaway line can shatter still-water thoughts, fragmenting them into a kaleidoscope of confusion. Hello. This is your life. Wake up. Look. Turquoise and sapphire. Shimmering crimson and gold. This is you. Or that is you. Change it. Twist it. You could be anything.

Hell. She'd been fine all these years. Just dusting, pottering really, cooking dinners and watching TV. Not thinking. And now this. Bam!

Helen tried to recall what it was Rita had actually said but couldn't. All that remained was an imprint and besides it barely mattered because already she had moved to the planning stage, propelled by hormones laid dormant, muddied and slothful, now stirred up from the bottom of the pond by an invisible hand. And the child was becoming real to her, solid as her own flesh, warm as her beating heart, smelling of vanilla and almonds, of talcum powder and biscuits, large brown eyes full of wonder...

The man needed to be tall, of athletic build with dark hair and brown eyes like Richard. Preferably known to her - family history, mental stability, things like that. Helen looked across the dinner table at Richard chewing methodically through his venison grill. At what point had his masterful silence become simply selfish? His brooding darkness, greying and withered? The demands petulant, the orders irritating?

She pushed the remains of her meal aside and sprang up, avoiding looking at the inevitable sulk pulling down the corners of his mouth while she told him about Pip and Jonathon's tennis bash a week next Sunday. She began spooning up dessert even though he hadn't finished his main course. It was only down the road but he wouldn't want to go. Neither would she normally, but the kaleidoscope had turned and now tantalising colours danced before her, dazzling in their brilliance, changing and re-arranging, dropping into place until images became shapes. And then one shape. Adam.

Adam, Pip's strapping twenty-three year old son, with dark curly hair and wide brown eyes. And Adam, with his easy smile and rather naughty penchant for older women, would be perfect. A tiny thrill began to fizz around inside her.

Richard had never wanted children. Fifteen years older with two grown-up daughters from a previous marriage - one never spoke to him, the other had a trail of debts he periodically picked up - he'd been adamant from the start. And at the time Helen hadn't minded, swept away by Richard's smouldering, largely unspent passion. A man who loved her, took care of her and dreamed the same dreams. But that was then. And this was twenty years later. Now he spent Sunday afternoons weeding the vegetable patch, his evenings reading the broadsheets and his scant conversations muttering about pension plans or leaky guttering.

She wasn't ready to be old. Not yet. And especially not now - with this...this...new found possibility. For it *was* possible. And the yearning, once acknowledged, became a cavernous void that must be filled. Her mind began to chatter incessantly day and night. She thrashed around under the heat of the bedclothes, waking at four or five, tired and tearful. A brown eyed boy. He would never know. Two men. Same night. And if she didn't do this? What of her life? The kaleidoscope stopped, that's what, the screen blank and white. Silence. Nothing. So then, she had her answer.

Adam would be at his parents' summer party - barbeque, drinks, games and music. The dates were perfect - bang in the middle of her cycle. But, and here was the tricky bit - how to approach her neighbour's son? Once, about a year ago and to her enormous chagrin, they had exchanged a shy smile. Confident beyond his years he'd mouthed a silent, "hi!" and she'd flushed deeply as his wide-set, foxy brown eyes swept impertinently down her body. Once though. Could she, on that flimsy basis, risk everything? And would he want her? And where?

Helen's hormones bubbled and popped, surging through her veins like passengers on a runaway roller coaster holding gleefully onto the sides of their little cart, oblivious to all rational thought. Richard? Don't think. Pip? Would be happy for her. A late baby. How wonderful. Her mother? Don't think. In swooped the image to blank out all others - a sweet, warm child to hold in her arms. A pram with a frilly, white cotton canopy that billowed in the breeze. Soft, fleecy blankets and fluffy toys. Tiny pink toes and fingers that curled around hers refusing to let go.

The days ticked by, painful and slow. She flicked through novels with pages unseen, stared at television programmes while her mind skittered elsewhere. Would

Adam even be there? And what was she going to say? What if he laughed at her? Or worse, insulted her? Cold fear poured into hot blood as carefully she picked out the clothes she would wear. Something - oh the burning shame - to entice and seduce.

When the time came it was a hot Sunday afternoon in late August, dry and airless, with heat shimmering off parched grass verges and tarmac lying in syrupy pools. Already sticky with perspiration, they wandered round to the back of Pip and Jonathon's large Victorian semi. To a scene of such startling, surreal Englishness their presence felt like an intrusion: floral frocks, Pimms on ice, bursts of laughter and the thwack of tennis balls. On court, Adam was busy smashing these at a couple of shrieking teenage girls on the other side of the net.

Helen, after kissing Pip on the cheek and accepting a drink, flitted restlessly from group to group, murmuring pleasantries to old people in hats, plump ladies with pink knees and sunburned shoulders and jolly ex-army types sweating in blazers, all the while trying to quell her rising panic.

At one point she was cornered by Tom, Pip's landscape gardener, a man with weathered skin and dancing blue eyes in an elfin face. "Come and see my dahlias," he said suggestively and laughed. Helen smiled distractedly while shooting a darting glance towards the tennis court - the game had ended - at Adam, muscles gleaming like a horse after a race, hands raking through glossy, dark curls, out of breath, panting…

"Stop it," she heard a silly, flirtatious voice say to Tom. Or was it to herself? "Behave yourself." She was watching Adam make his way indoors. The planning stage was over. It was time for the execution.

Inside, Pip's house seemed dark with curtains drawn against the inferno heat. She heard the shower clunk to a halt and began to make her way upstairs, hands gripping the banister to stop them from shaking. He would be half naked, a towel around his waist, still pumping endorphins after his game. They would meet at the top of the stairs and she would say…Oh God, what would she say? Useless thoughts about the shopping list and snippets from the book she was reading tumbled over each other as she climbed. Almost there. Suddenly the bathroom door flew open and her heart slammed against her chest.

Adam, two steps above her, glanced down, taking in her open buttons and milky white cleavage. An expression of raw hunger travelled across his young features. Unmistakeable. It had to be now. With his flat, glistening stomach at eye level. Just a damp towel. His room - a boy's room with dirty socks on the floor and posters on the wall. Door ajar. Dark. No one would know. Minutes, that was all…

A voice cut through the air. "Adam! Hurry up will you? Chloe and Emma are here." They turned. And the moment withered and died. For God's sake she was his mother's best friend. Looking back she saw him smile - regretfully? - and rather disconcertingly, shrug, before sauntering into his bedroom and kicking the door shut behind him.

Nausea rose in her throat as she scurried into the steamy bathroom, hanging over the sink. She'd almost done it. Whatever had she been thinking? How utterly and completely mad. Fate had stepped in. Must have. Fractured arguments exchanged in rapid fire: look, she'd been saved; Richard would have had apoplexy; the marriage finished. She turned on the tap and began to splash her face: accept it; so disappointed; don't you dare cry; all over…a middle aged fool…And then out of the corner of her eye she saw the doorknob turn.

She stood totally still, hot tears stinging her eyes, vaguely aware of music drifting up from the garden - pumping stuff that picked up the heartbeat and thumped it through veins. And when she looked up he was standing there.

The need was instant and blinding. The act savage. And afterwards they lay panting, sweat melding skin together, limbs entwined on Pip's bathmat.

Surprisingly she found it rather easy to return to the party. Easier than before to make small talk and, with the job done and relief washing through her body in torrents, a positive joy to acquiesce when Richard, reeking of alcohol, lurched over and said, "Come on, let's go. Had enough."

Their lovemaking that evening, as ever, would be brief and wordless. She had secretly tried to time his intermittent urges with her cycle but his silent heaves had produced nothing. Nor ever would.

And as the weeks and months passed and she began to show, a strange calmness dampened the flighty adrenalin that had ricocheted around her body for so long. Now she lay in bed in the mornings and sat dreamily through entire meals. The kaleidoscope turned from this way to that, from luscious fuchsia and coral to startling gold and orange, then finally to the black and white of winter. Soon the colours would turn again and it would be spring. And then she would have to tell Richard. The man she had once loved so much. Not about his miracle brown eyed boy. But the child with the dancing blue eyes and the elfin face.

A new life beckoned. Not the one she'd planned. Different.

9

OUT OF THE WOODS

Jack felt himself being watched as he locked the church door. Turning, he squinted into the low, winter sun and noticed a familiar figure leaning against one of the gravestones. Although eighteen years had passed since he had last seen him, Toby had never really gone away - haunting his thoughts and possessing his nightmares as if everything had happened only yesterday.

Their eyes locked and darkness rushed in like heat from an oven: *tangled branches, rapid breathing, pounding feet. Solid black, couldn't see, stumbling, on his knees, up again, running and running...*

"Tobes," he said, with a forced smile. "Long time no see. How're things?"

Toby's dark eyes searched his own, touching a deep, dark secret, painfully wrenching it free. Jack quelled a rise of nausea.

"It's time, Jack," said Toby quietly. "This thing isn't going to go away."

Jack tried to still the jackhammer beat of his heart, his voice barely a whisper. "What is it? What's happened?"

"It's Leo. My son. He's acting weird, saying things. Jack, it's impossible but - he knows. He knows everything."

"He can't."

"We have to talk." Toby indicated his car.

The wind was whipping up, granite clouds scudding over them fast and low. Jack dipped his head as he plodded after Toby. *Nothing good was going to come of today.* Moments later they were sitting in Toby's comfortably upholstered Volvo Estate, baby-seat in the back, tissues and half eaten bags of sweets evidence of a normal family life. Jack pressed his fingers to his temples. Eighteen years and not a word of contact. Eighteen years of professionalism, of prayer and atonement - of waking in the small hours soaked in sweat, the subconscious surfacing nightly to remind him. And now this. Of course, of course they would have to pay. How could they go forward as respectable professionals - he a priest, Toby a doctor - after what they'd done? It was Judgement Day and he had always known it would come.

Toby sighed heavily. The last time the two of them had spoken had been in similar circumstances. As teenagers in Toby's white van - sitting on scuffed, torn seats with bits of foam spilling out, Jack staring straight ahead and Toby slumped over the steering wheel. The smell of sweat and fear hung heavily in the air after spending most of the weekend in the police station.

"You didn't tell them anything, did you?" said Toby.

"Of course not."

They would later go home and shower until their skins burned, scrubbing and scrubbing as if it was possible to cleanse their souls into shiny new things again instead of what they now were - dirty, rotten, debased.

The interrogation had been relentless for both, going round and round in circles with neither of them saying anything other than they couldn't remember. It was supposed to have been a laugh. A camping trip. And when they woke up Marilyn had gone.

After an interminable silence Toby cleared his throat. "It's Leo…he's… "

A strong gust of wind rattled the car and a shower of golden leaves scattered across the bonnet.

Jack's stomach tightened. The afternoon was darkening already, unnaturally so. "Go on."

"God knows I've tried to do the right things in life…" Toby raked his hair into a rooster look. "…worked hard, look after my patients, my family… But it's not going to go away. It's started all over again."

"What is it about Leo?" Jack prompted.

"Yeah, my eldest. Fine, absolutely fine - bright, healthy, sociable. Then he turned thirteen and well, Eve noticed it first - things being moved around in his room. She'd put a pile of towels down on his bed and when she came back they'd be in the middle of the floor - things like that. Odd noises in the night - the computer flashing up, TV switching itself on. And then one morning he told me clear and calm as you like that he knew what I'd done. And he knew where Marilyn was."

"But you'd never told him. Never told anyone, right? Not even Eve."

"Of course bloody not. Are you mad?" He raked his hair again into a cockatoo. Then turned and looked right into Jack's eyes. Holding the moment. Steady and dark. "Jack - I think he's possessed. By Marilyn."

Jack swallowed a rise of nausea as he tried to make sense of the information. Marilyn was his sister. And the way she had died, horrifically disturbing. "Why? I mean, how do you know it's her?"

"He speaks in her voice. Only to me. At night when

something happens and he wakes up in a panic. I'll rush in and then he changes from frightened boy to this malicious girl in the flick of a light switch. Jack - it's her: she does that thing with her hair - you know, flicking it back? And bats her eyelashes at me - with my son's face! And then out comes this low, seductive voice."

"Saying what?"

"Saying she's watching us both and the truth will out."

"You're seriously telling me that my dead sister is speaking through Leo?"

"That's what I am seriously telling you. And I'm also seriously telling you that it's true because he told me exactly where Marilyn was and he's right."

Jack opened the door and hurried onto the grass where he vomited, then stood panting, sweating, propped against the yew tree with one hand while Toby waited and watched from the warmth of his car. Maybe Toby was mad, the guilt finally getting to him. Yet something told him no, after what he had witnessed all those years ago this was possible. And worse, there was more to come. He quickly recited a short prayer. He would need all his strength because, dear God, Toby wanted something from him. And he knew what it would be.

***

His sister, Marilyn, had always been trouble. They should never in a million light years have let her persuade them. It was Toby's fault - something going on between them.

"Come on you pair of lightweights. It's just a laugh. A teeny-weeny little séance in the woods. We can tell the parents it's just a camping trip. Cathy's up for it, Jack!"

He'd had a thing for Cathy with her baby-blonde hair and wide blue eyes, a girl who did whatever Marilyn told her to. He'd wavered. Felt manipulated. Changed his mind back again. "No way."

"Come on - I've got the Ouija Board," Marilyn said, green eyes dancing with excitement. "It'll be such a laugh."

And then she played her Ace. Sidling up to Toby she'd whispered in his ear and Toby had grinned like an oaf. His sister had long, black hair and a body she flaunted in tight, revealing clothes. She liked to watch the effect she had on the boys, husbands, fathers...

Even when Cathy dropped out at the last minute on some pathetic excuse Toby was still keen. "Come on mate, just a camping trip. Let her do her spooky stuff if she wants. I've got some cans and some E's."

So he'd gone with them. A gooseberry in petulant mood.

Once they'd set up camp at the far end of the woods near to where the new bypass was being built, Marilyn had triumphantly produced a bottle of vodka and the Ouija board. The night had been the blackest he could ever remember - no moon, no stars and no wind to hurry along the thick, grey clouds that hung wet and low. Late autumn, the air was smoky and cold already, the leaves beneath them brown and soggy. They lit a fire and Marilyn positioned candles in a circle. All they could see was each other's faces, bobbing eerily above dark clothes, alight with excitement and fear and ghoulish life in the deadened woods, that waited still and dark behind them.

Closing his eyes, Jack could still see Marilyn's sly grin and taunting eyes, her hair hanging long and loose as she stared at his friend with open intent.

Jack took a tissue from his coat pocket, dabbed at his face, then slowly walked back to the car.

"What are we going to do, then?"

"Eve wants him to go to a psychiatrist, but then of course she would, she doesn't know the history. He's not ill, though, Jack. This is your department. You're a priest. We can't let him start talking - bringing it up. Someone might investigate. Jack - we have no choice. You have to exorcise him."

He knew this was coming. Yet still his stomach flipped and pinheads of sweat rose across his forehead. "I've never done one."

"Time to start. We can't let him talk. He's getting more and more insistent. He was very precise."

Jack said nothing.

"I thought we were out of the woods. God, I've spent most of my life never doing anything wrong ever again - I don't drop so much as a sweet wrapper."

Jack nodded. How he had prayed and prayed for forgiveness.

"And what good would it do for us to go to prison now? We're valuable, respectable professionals. People need us, look up to us. What good would it do?"

Jack nodded again. "And Leo needs help."

"Yes," said Toby. "He does."

"Damn Mariliyn"

The car shook in a particularly violent gust and leaves whirled frantically in a multitude of circles.

"Let's do it, then," said Toby.

***

"It's called 'Listen to the Glass,' Marilyn explained.

The three of them put their hand on the upturned wineglass and at first nothing happened. They each popped an E and passed around the lager.

Then the wineglass began to shoot around the Ouija board and the woods around them stilled to an eerie silence. Not a single leaf rustled, nor twig snapped. No owls hooted and not a creature stirred in the undergrowth. It was as if life itself dared not breathe.

The fire flared and the candles burned brighter and brighter. Marilyn's laugh rang loud and shrill. She opened the vodka and poured it down her throat, letting it spill onto her top so Toby could see she had nothing on underneath. "Is there a spirit with us?" she asked in a mocking voice.

The glass shot to YES.

Marilyn passed round the vodka and they all took long gulps, enjoying the burn that hit their stomachs.

"WHO?"

M A R I L Y N

Without warning a hiking boot flew across the board and into the trees behind.

"Shit," said Jack.

Marilyn was thrilled. "It works, it works!" Tipping more vodka down her throat, she wiped her full, blood red mouth with the back of her hand and grinned. "Do you mean us harm?" she asked, with a giggle.

The boys looked at each other, ashen faced. "Let's stop now, Marilyn."

But again the glass flew: YES

And then it took a life of its own, rocketing around the board: B I T C H,

G E T O U T, L E A V E.

The air closed in rapidly like a wall - a heavy, cloying scent reminiscent of rotting flowers filling their lungs and clouding their eyes. The smoke thickened. A strong wind whipped up, making the flames leap ever higher. Then suddenly the board flew into the air and this was where events blurred. Marilyn - jumping up, swathed in flames, her hair on fire, screaming…

***

Toby, Jack and Leo headed into the woods with rucksacks and provisions for a weekend of fishing and games. This time the night was lit by a waning moon and a hazy galaxy of stars. Their breath steamed in the cold, night air as they tramped deeper and deeper towards the centre. They could not, Jack said, afford to be discovered.

"Not where we were before though, eh?" said Toby, flinching every time an owl hooted or a twig cracked.

"No."

But once amongst the trees their bearings became muddled and it wasn't long before the roar of the bypass could be heard.

"Too far," said Toby. "Let's backtrack a bit."

"You've been here before, haven't you?" said Leo.

Open mouthed, both men turned to look at him. Both denied it.

Leo shrugged but he kept looking at his father with darkening eyes until Toby looked away. He rubbed his hands together, pretending a paternal confidence and jollity he didn't feel. "Right. Let's go further back, nearer the stream and then set up camp before it gets too dark, eh?"

Running faster than the heartbeat, clawing at branches, gripping onto the weight in the sheet that slipped and slithered, fingers of darkness clutching at their clothes, nearly there, panting, chest hurting, lungs bursting…

After supper, with the fire flickering, Jack suggested a game of cards. If he tried hard enough he could make himself believe this really was a camping trip with an old mate and his boy. But there was a weight pressing in, making his lungs feel leaden, making it harder to breathe. He looked over his shoulder. Darkness had descended like the blackest curtain, chasing away all vestiges of daylight and bringing with it ancient fears from the beginning of time - of everything unknown, of powers unseen that could bring madness and destroy souls. The lit candle of faith deep within him flickered and faltered. This would be his ultimate test.

"Coffee?" suggested Toby.

"God, yes." Jack took a grateful sip. He must help Leo. Help them all. He must not, could not, fail "Leo - you know I'm a priest?"

Leo nodded.

"Your dad says you've been feeling a bit disturbed recently about some of the things that have been happening and I'd like to say a little prayer over you. Get rid of whatever it is that's troubling you. Would that be okay?"

Leo nodded. "Is that why you got me here? To stop all the weird stuff going on?"

Jack smiled. "Partly. And we wanted an excuse for a camping trip, of course - away from the girls and all that." Flashing into his mind came the distorted, screaming face of his mother eighteen years ago, together with the aching, empty feeling that dogged the rest of his years. The only sound came from the stream - trickling over rocks and pebbles, bubbling and gurgling like a party of voices - hypnotic, soothing, powerful. Tony and Leo were waiting.

Jack blessed the holy water he had brought with him and was about to begin the prayer when Leo said in

Marilyn's low, husky voice, "What did you do with the board, Jack?"

Toby jolted visibly.

"Pardon?" said Jack.

"The Ouija board," said Leo, batting his eyelashes. "What did you do with it? Because if you burnt it then the evil spirit you raised will stay around forever. You'll never get rid of it."

***

It had taken what seemed like hours but eventually Jack and Toby had managed to put out the blaze. Marilyn had burst into an immediate and ferocious inferno. Within seconds the fireball was white-hot and even though they had frantically grabbed ground sheets to throw over her, it was too late. They rolled her

body back and forth in the damp, autumn leaves until there was nothing left but the night, a blackened corpse and the smell of burning flesh.

They'd stood gasping for breath, choking from the smoke, red, stinging eyes staring with horror at the sight before them.

Jack sank to his knees, pushing his fist into his mouth to stop himself from screaming.

The wind had dropped to nothing and the woods were still and silent again.

"We have to bury her," said Toby. "Quick, think, think. Nobody in the world will believe what happened. Did you see it? Did you see the flames go crazy like that?"

Jack had been too numb to speak, too petrified to move. *Nobody would believe them. The night had been still. She was dead. His sister was dead.* In the end he'd let himself be told what to do, had done what Toby suggested and rolled Marilyn's body, which was little more than blackened bones and dripping sinews, back into the sheet.

And then they'd run like wild animals from guns, racing over rocks and streams, tripping over gnarled roots, falling into ditches, branches scratching at their eyes. The new bypass was near, the site deserted and the foundations for the bridge deep. "Drop her down there and the bridge will go on top," said Toby. "Come on, Jack, we *have* to do it. *We have to.*"

Then emerging from the woods in the early hours, they'd told the world that they had woken up to find Marilyn gone. Vanished.

When Eve arrived home the following day she was surprised to see a police officer waiting for her. Bundling the younger children inside, she demanded to know what had happened. Beyond her, peering out of the patrol car was the sooty, tired looking face of her son, Leo. Found, the police officer told her, stumbling along the roadside near to the local beauty spot, a wooded area on the edge of town.

"So what happened? Where are Toby and his friend?"

The police officer inclined his head towards the house. "I think perhaps we should go indoors. The boy says they disappeared. He woke up and they'd gone. Vanished."

"What?"

"We have to take him in for questioning, obviously. In the meantime, may I ask if you and your husband were having difficulties? If perhaps there was somewhere he was planning on going? A relative, a friend....?"

Eve, wild-eyed, distracted, shook her head. "No." She looked over his shoulder to Leo in the car.

He looked back calmly. And very faintly, smiled.

10

THE CHASE

He's there in my rear view mirror. He knows I've seen him. I can tell by the way he leans into the steering wheel, accelerating hard, pulling out at the last moment so he's close. Really close. Close enough to stare across his passenger seat for several intense seconds before speeding off. He does it over and over. The man in the black Range Rover. And it sends a thrill right through me.

My name is Marla. I'm in with the big boys now. I always knew I'd be one of those super cool businesswomen with a show-off car and killer heels. You know - wowing them in the board room, every man fantasising about what I'm wearing underneath my tight, black suit. And here I am. Well you've got to start somewhere haven't you? I've got this sapphire blue Beamer with alloy wheels and satnav. The others can't stand it - the other regulars, that is.

It's like zooming down the motorway on a high speed sofa, getting your own reality TV show - there's Madman behind me right now for instance, doing over 100 mph with a broadsheet spread out across the dashboard. He must be less than three feet away from my rear bumper. *And* he's on the phone. Jesus! I pull quickly into the middle lane, pulse pumping hard, hand held up to the car I've swerved in front of. And sure enough I've pissed off Fiona Fiesta. Now FF really doesn't like me one bit. She's always here around this time on a Friday.

"Bitch!" she mouths, her face contorted with rage. Now I'm for it. I know what FF is like for holding a grudge and believe me this charade is going to continue for the next two junctions. For the kick-off she'll drive up real close, then overtake and draw level so I can see her sticking up her finger and spitting obscenities. Then she'll veer in front and slam on her brakes.

I touch my rear view mirror to let her know I'm aware the game has begun. I will win. I can accelerate away any time I like, and that's what we both know is at the root of the problem here - a blonde in a brand new, super shiny BMW - a company car. I smile. I'm safe. And stick up one perfectly manicured finger.

Once the game is over it's like the lights have gone out. I'm bored again, left to the drone of the road and the irritating tedium of Ken Bruce. I picture him as a bearded uncle in a patterned sweater, parked on the family sofa all weekend with his copy of the Guardian, teasing you in a way he imagines is amusing. You try to humour him but your face freezes, you've lost the will to live...

Junction 23 - is that all? Ah, here's Rat boy. Rat boy in a clapped out red Peugeot, wearing a baseball cap backwards, stereo system bouncing his car off the tarmac. Bumf, bumf, bumf... Thinks he's cool, weaving in and out like he has the last word in smart driving. Look at him - mean, ferret mouth, white claws gripping the steering wheel. And he's making headway until we hit road works - the cones - and then he's stuffed because no one, absolutely no one will let him in. He disappears, a red dot in my mirror. And I smile.

Once past the cones, in the two lane crawl through the road works I peel a banana. I'm just pushing the fleshy fruit into my mouth when I become aware of being watched. Hell. I'm level with Range Rover man. How undignified. Quickly I take a huge bite and stuff the rest of it into the door pocket, surreptitiously getting a better look at this guy in my wing mirror - US marine style, close-cropped silver hair, deep tan, and a row of sharp, white teeth fixed in a knowing grin. Big shoulders, short-sleeved shirt, large square fingers. His Range Rover roars as he levels, pulls ahead, drops back, flicking little glances my way. Boy is he interested. Well you can look all you like, buster. I'm safe. This is such a game. I love it.

It's then I decide to do something I've never done before - take things just that teeny weeny step further. A spur of the moment thing really. I look right across at him, giving him a come-on smile. He smiles back and for one tantalising moment our sunglasses meet, mouths curved into watermelon slices. He points at the services ahead and makes the sign 'T'.

Holy shit. Hang on a minute. I can't actually meet with him. He looks like someone's husband, a big man, older than my dad. Did he expect... Oh my God... I'm well... God, do people actually do things like that? The traffic is breaking free and I rocket off. He's right behind me, though. And I mean right behind. Bumper to bumper. He's pointing to the Services. Look mate, I was just playing, okay? It was just a joke.

A glance at the speedo - 110 mph. I slow down to 80. So does he. I cut across three lanes to the inside. So does he.

His mouth is set in a tight grimace. He looks angry.

Who is he? I envisage his life - mock Tudor mansion on an upmarket estate, two kids, wife a primary school teacher, plays golf…Takes risks with a woman he doesn't know because he feels like it. In a Service Station car park… It's gone all sordid and sleazy and I don't like it. Not one bit. I'm only twenty- two. Give me a break.

Junction 11 and my bladder's so full it feels like a cow's udder after a day's grazing - it hurts, swelling up into a balloon. *I've got to stop*. There's a Services ahead. Need to lose him. Foot down hard. Veering across three lanes and into the fast one - up to 100mph. He's right behind me. There's a lorry blocking the middle lane but I must get off. Think! Quickly… So what I do is this - with no warning or signal, swerve in front of the lorry then swoop up the slip road and into the Services, leaving him with no option but to sail past.

Smooth or what? The look of shock on his face was priceless. Still, my knees are trembling slightly when I step out into the petrol-fumed air.

The women's white-tiled toilets are freezing, the floor still wet from a recent mopping. It's like dropping into an asylum. Shivering, I quickly wash my hands and take a reality check in the black-spotted mirror. With the sunglasses off my eyes whites are pink from an early start. Always happens. And my hair hangs bedraggled either side of my face, like an Afghan hound some bitch once said. I wonder if I should eat my mum's sandwiches in the car or have something here. Range Rover man is long gone - probably twenty miles South by now. God that was a close call.

The car park is full when I emerge, traffic hurtling past in a thunderous race. I'm darting to my car, still exhilarated at the sight of it - mine, all mine - glancing at my watch - two hours to get to Head Office for my presentation - when I spot it. A gleaming black Range Rover in the corner by the picnic area, a pair of reflective sunglasses and a barracuda smile. Christ. I'm in the car with the locks on in less than a second. I'm out of here, tyres screeching, sunglasses half on, joining the motorway amid a blast of horns. Up to 70 mph, 80. 90.

He's right behind me.

Okay, now I have to keep calm. There's nothing he can do. The next stop is Head Office. I have central locking, half a tank. And yet - a quick check in the rear view mirror and I can see his mouth set in a hard line of fury. So this is how it happens - abduction, rape, murder - lurid headlines, another luckless girl. I'm running through a forest barefoot, stumbling, twisting my ankle - he's gaining on me, laughing, knowing he will win in the end. I'm screaming. I'm crying. How I wish I'd never read Patricia Cornwell.

No, stop it. Think positive. I'm not a little girl, I'm a business woman and I'm not taking any shit from anyone.

Mum's sandwiches lie on the passenger seat. She's made me chicken and tomato, my favourite, and I'm going to eat them. Calmly. In civilised Britain. On my ninety mile an hour sofa. He's swigging from a can of coke. I watch, chewing, swallowing, slowing down to seventy. He leans forward to adjust something - his radio? - probably something controlled, almost surgical like Mozart. And my stomach clenches.

We're coming into London. The whole feel of everything changes. It's no longer the grey North, but a pink tinged world of promise - here is where it all happens. I can do anything. Anything. Expertly I zip through the maze of interlinks to the North Circular, cutting people up with precision. He's hot on my tail. Oh God. He's not going to let this go, is he?

We're at the traffic lights now. Through my mirror I can see curly, grey hairs poking through his open-neck shirt. He stares straight ahead. Maybe it's all over. Is it? And then he raises a single finger and points. A cold drop in the pit of my stomach and I sit up straight. Every synapse firing, adrenaline bouncing off my organs like a game of bagatelle. He's going to follow me and grab me, isn't he? Oh no, oh no...What the hell have I gone and done?

We're moving off. I almost collide with the car in front from staring at him in the rear view mirror. Brake. He hasn't hit me. Saw it coming. Laughs. Mirror, mirror - tell me this isn't true. My turn off is coming up on the left. Any time now. Please, oh please, next time I look let him not be there. There is only Head Office and a park on this road for miles. If he turns off here I know he's coming for me.

I start to make the turn. He draws level. For an instant. Then smiles and waves, giving a little parp of the horn before shooting straight ahead.

Relief washes through me in torrents. I realise I've been sweating profusely, rivulets of fear running down my back, sticking my palms to the steering wheel, plastering my blouse to my skin. I check my rear view mirror - nothing. A white van. Then a courier. He's gone.

11

GIRL IN THE RAIN

She was thumbing a lift on the A1 slip road when I first saw her: mini skirt, long, dark hair dripping down her back, tramping along in the pouring rain with a cigarette clamped between heavily ringed fingers and a rucksack on her shoulder.

Don't pick her up.

The Merc was easing into fourth and I shouldn't have stopped, but something about the kid's sopping clothes and the HGVs thundering past, showering her with muddy spray on what was a mercilessly cold, squally November night, nagged at my conscience.

"Where do you want to go?"

She shrugged, pale face bobbing through my zapped down window. "Anywhere." She was shivering in a thin, cheap pink parka, arms hugging her chest, bare legs covered in goose pimples.

The Merc's seats were cream leather so I grabbed my Mac off the back seat and spread it for her to sit on. "I'm going as far as Darlington if that's any good to you?" *Mistake.*

She nodded, stubbed out what remained of her cigarette on the wet road and slid into the warm, luxurious cocoon of my car.

"Soon have you warmed up," I said, turning up the

heater as she rubbed her arms, rivulets of water running down her legs into scuffed trainers. "I'm Janine, by the way. You?"

"Leah." She smelled of chips.

"Do you like Miles Davis?" Miles' cool, lazy jazz snaked out of the CD player like curls of smoke, conjuring up images of the end of a party, waking bleary-eyed to find everyone else had gone and the cleaners had arrived.

Leah shrugged. "Whatever." She'd got her texting fingers poised over the mobile she'd instantly plucked from the rucksack, leaving a trail of lip gloss, crisp packets and tissues strewn across my immaculately valeted carpet.

The rain was gaining momentum, drumming methodically on the roof, wipers swatting furiously at road spray - a never-ending car wash. Leah's phone beep-beeped and she read the latest text message while dabbing at her legs with a tissue; her tiny skirt a sodden dishrag clinging to mottled thighs.

"Hardly dressed for it," I said.

"Whatever."

Dan can't stand girls like her. Gum popping, cigarette sucking, monosyllabic teens who dress like hookers. The thought of him and how near I was to him, getting closer with every minute, kick started my heart, taking me by surprise. People were driving too slowly. "For God's sake - it's only a bit of rain." Too close to the lorry in front, I couldn't see properly, pulled out, 70mph, up to 80, 90... I could feel Dan's rage building up already. See his face glaring out at the rain lashed night... I picked up a hitchhiker. I'm sorry. I shouldn't have done it. Mistake.

It had been a long day, showcasing illustrations and

marketing ideas for an advertising company. My profession and I'm proud of it - gives me a sense of who I am and what I could be. But freelance. Best that way. I can only cope with one boss and that's Dan. *Never forget it. Don't ever forget.* Red taillights reflected off the road; blurred faces at windows, everyone trying to get home. Time, so little of it.

Leah stopped texting and looked across at me, at my face screwed up in concentration, at my hands, claw like, on the steering wheel. "In a hurry?"

"I just have to get home, that's all."

"Husband?"

I chose to ignore her. Why should I tell this irresponsible girl anything? Besides, I don't talk about Dan. "You?" I nodded towards the mobile phone she appeared to be welded to. "Boyfriend trouble?"

"Yeah, right."

"Ex-boyfriend then?" *Mistake number two. Don't get her talking.*

"Shagged some stupid tart, didn't he? I mean, ohmyGod, what a total slapper…"

The rain was really coming down by then, pounding the car, and the last place I wanted to be in weather like that was stuck in a metal box. Locked in. Because the memories start creeping back - just me and the rain hammering on a corrugated iron roof, all night, in the blackness with the spiders and their webs catching at my hair, damp seeping into my bones, tiredness warring with fear until the fear is all there is. Hugging myself, wondering what is worse - the dark or the emergence of dawn with its eerie grey fingers poking through the sooty window, and the sound of heavy boots clomping up the steps. "Lily? Lily…. Where are you?"

Like I said, I shouldn't have picked her up. Dan really hates girls like that, detests the sexual bravado, the slovenly self-satisfaction. I knew he'd be livid. And increasingly Dan's rage is more than I can bear. It drains me, leaving me limp as a rag doll, a victim, useless and helpless with no one coming to make it better, no one to take away the pain... And I can see him, watching and waiting, feel his temper rising, know what's coming.

"So we was at this club, yeah? And Darren says to Carla..."

Leah was smearing on lip gloss like she was going to a party or something, and I could see my leather seats were wet where she'd carelessly let the coat slip. *Get rid of her. You know what's going to happen...*

The trickle of memories became a flood - a creaking door, a shaft of light and a silhouette. Hands that reach down and haul me to my feet by my hair, hands that ball into fists, that slap and tear clothes. The same hands that cajole and stroke and wipe away the tears...

But Dan and I can never be parted. It's way too late now. We've come this far, and besides he'd hunt me down, track me like a poacher outwitting prey. I will never be free. There was no such thing as a safe house for me back then and there isn't now. Not when the enemy is within. I just have to stop the rage, not give him a reason, control things. And get rid of this stupid, vacuous girl.

"Look, Leah, I need to drop you here." There was a Services up ahead - not a great one, admittedly, with HGVs lined up outside and a flashing neon sign over a truckers' café - but a haven nonetheless.

She looked up from texting. "Oh great."

I could picture Dan shaking his head, jaw hardening. "She said what? Ungrateful bitch."

"Sorry. Look, I have to turn off soon anyway and you can get a coffee here until the rain stops." *Just go.*

The Merc glided into a car park that had to be one of the saddest places on earth - petroleum laced puddles, men with beer bellies looking out through rain smeared windows into a night they couldn't see - and left her there. A stick figure with mascara smudged eyes sticking up one single, defiant finger at my retreating lights.

Well I'm sorry, but I couldn't think about her anymore. I had to get home and fast. Foot down hard, I swung the car out across both lanes amid a cacophony of horn blowing. Dan, Dan, I'm sorry…I shouldn't have. I was so close, almost home, almost there. I glanced at the clock on the dashboard - eight-thirty. Not so bad. There was time yet, time to deal with him, to control the situation. Surely. If only I hadn't picked up that girl, slowed down, chatted…if only it hadn't been raining.

Signs for Darlington materialised out of the gloom. The rain was easing off, giving way to chasing clouds and buffeting winds. A long, empty road and then suburbia with its neat lawns and closed curtains, ordinary people tucked up safe and warm. Our house is large and stone built, the driveway lined with cedars that bent and bounced in the gusts that shook them, ghostly shrubs quivering on the lawn, rivers of rainwater washing mushy, yellow leaves down the tarmac, bubbling out of drains and dripping from gutters.

I put my key in the lock. Turned it. And stepped into the silent, darkened hallway.

The onslaught was vicious. One of the worst. Filthy, mangled words of hatred, paintings ripped from walls, glass shattered, the release of a pent up fury that left me shaking, hands and arms covering my head, tears streaming down my face, hugging myself, rocking and pleading for it to stop.

Later - how much I couldn't say, so lost the hours that strung together in fitful, restless dreams - that all too familiar feeling, clutching an empty bottle of vodka, peering out from the hair strewn across my eyes and listening to the clatter of milk bottles. I heard the clunk of the letterbox and raised my aching head. Another day. A grey, washed out kind of brightness. Coffee. Papers. Deadlines to meet.

The photo that stared up at me from the tabloid was a bit of a jolt. Leah - a smiling schoolgirl of 15 had been a runaway. The first time she'd ever left home, both parents frantic. She'd been found badly beaten but alive somewhere off the A1 near Scotch Corner. Alive though. That was the thing.

My distorted reflection in the stainless steel fridge looked back at me with a strangely triumphant expression. So, Dan, you didn't get this one, did you? Janine got home in time. Got rid of the girl before the rage set in. I laughed, a sound that rang hollow and hung in the air like the ghost of a child. Lily. The little girl covered in bruises who lives inside me, protected by Janine. I keep all three of us locked in. Only sometimes I forget how strong he is and Dan breaks out, killing the type of girls he hates with that rage of ours. Leah got lucky. I really shouldn't pick them up.

12
THE LAST BUS HOME

The bus chugs home like so many times before. And Ruby, pale face staring out into the black night, is thinking about Lewis. About marrying him. About tonight and how he bought her an engagement ring and what her dad's going to say about that.

She twiddles the cheap, silver plated ring as the bus lurches to a halt and the remaining two passengers stumble down the steps, pulling their coats around them as they face the howling wind and vanish into the darkness. Ruby's stop is the last one and there are many miles to go yet.

She closes her eyes and dreams of Lewis, of his lovely, golden-skinned smile as he waved her off from the bus station, the town still buzzing with lights and pumping with music. He'd probably go back to the pub for a last half, maybe onto a club. She tries to quell the rising irritation. The fact that her family has to live right out here in the wilderness, far away from town where there are jobs and people and life. Here where there is nothing but sheep and thousands of acres covered in rocks, bogs and heather. Where the last bus home is at ten o'clock.

Lewis had kissed her hair and pulled her close. "Miss it," he whispered, his hands travelling down her back. "Stay with me."

The surge of response shook her. But no, not yet. Let her speak to Dad first.

Dad's face. She pictures the tightening of his mouth and the torn emotions in his soft, hazel eyes. Her mother's delight, then anxious bird-like glances, waiting for Dad's response. How is she going to phrase this for the best? Lewis works as a waiter in a downtown café - there is no way she can dress that up.

Finally she sees the lights of Moor End Farm bobbing in the gloom as the bus crawls ever higher, clunking into potholes, changing down a gear, heaving forwards again. Then the white mail box at the bottom of the drive, and as always her heart lifts at the sight of home, the pull strong - reminders of school days when she and her brothers would be the only kids left on the bus, eager to charge into the farmhouse kitchen to see what was cooking - maybe a batch of scones or a hot sponge.

Ruby reaches for her bag and buttons her coat, stands and begins to make her way towards the front of the bus. There's a slight dip as it levels with the farm gates and she holds tightly onto the pole, waiting for the screeching stop.

Except tonight the bus doesn't stop. Her heart jumps. Suddenly there is an almighty acceleration as the mail box flies past her line of vision.

"Hey! What's…"

The bus is careering into the night like a getaway vehicle at top speed, engines screaming, bouncing in and out of potholes. She crawls on her hands and knees, thrown violently from one side of the bus to the other, trying to grab onto a seat. The driver is chuckling. She hadn't noticed him when she got on with the crowd, expecting it would be old Percy, the only driver, presumably, who didn't mind spending his Saturday night chugging along the moors and back again. Only this isn't Percy.

She stares wide-eyed at the maniacal grin that turns her way. At the empty eyes and yellow tombstone teeth. There is a cold drop in the pit of her stomach. Blindly she lunges forwards to grab the steering wheel, hitting his head repeatedly with her bag. There is no plan, except nothing would be worse than being alone with this man on the moors, and at least this way there is a chance of escape. He's laughing louder and there is a wild frenzy of hair and hands until the bus suddenly hits a boulder and is thrown from the road.

For the longest time there is silence.

And then a sickening crunch. Over and over it rolls, glass smashing, metal crunching. And then it stops, hissing and steaming in the mud, rocks and gorse.

It is some time before Ruby, who has been thrown clear, opens her eyes. There are millions of stars in the jet sky. A fine mist scudding over a crescent moon. Her head hurts. And then she remembers. Nervously scans the area for signs of the driver.

A low moan - is it the wind sweeping the moors or is it him exhaling a ghastly breath? No time to lose. She has to get home. Fast. Several miles have been covered and it's a long way to walk, especially with the darkness so thick it almost breathes, like a life form closing in. She holds out her hands in front, testing each footfall for a pothole - expecting a grisly hand to grab her ankle - she must keep going. The mist will thicken quickly up here with visibility soon down to nothing.

Her hair soaks up the fine drizzle, dripping darkly down her back, thin dress clinging to her skin. But she will soon be home. She has lived here all the seventeen years of her life and knows every landmark from winters helping Dad rescue sheep, to exploring the moors with her brothers on their ponies and bikes, picnics packed for the day. Here now, the stone monolith claiming 15 miles to town. She grabs it, feeling the solid familiarity beneath her half-numb and bleeding fingers. Not long now. Keep going. She starts to sing. Softly at first. And then more loudly, "Early one morning, just as the sun was rising….." As if Dad will hear her and respond with his whistling, like he used to when she was little and had to come back alone on the bus in the dark. She would run down the long driveway, singing at the top of her voice and Dad would come out with his lantern, whistling, waiting for her. Ruby starts to cry.

And then, her insides skip and her heart picks up - the white mail box. She starts to run, stumbling forwards, hands stretched out ahead. She can see the mail box. It's there. Almost there. At last. "Mum! Dad!" She's shouting now. They must be worried, maybe out looking for her. It's been hours. Every little thing is passing through her mind - the first pony, a stocky, little piebald with a mind of his own - Dad leading her round and round the field on it when he was dead on his feet from lambing all day. And Mum insisting Ruby have her own private bedroom away from her brothers, painting it herself in sunshine yellow, giving her a copy of her first ever grown-up novel - 'I Capture the Castle,' by Dodie Smith. She still has the book, read so many times the pages are tissue thin.

"Mum! Dad!" The farmhouse is all darkness. Ruby hammers on the door, stumbling to the kitchen window. Home. Oh thank God she's home. She peers in - no-one there. They must be out searching for her. The

Landover's out. "Let me in! Anyone! Luke! Jason!"

But the tiredness. Like a weight pressing her down and down. She could sleep right here on the muddy yard. It takes the last of her energy - palms against the solid stone walls of the house, to find an open window. Scratching and scrabbling at the latch, she pushes herself through the narrow gap, landing like a slug into the gloomy house, crawls upstairs and throws herself onto the bed. Safety. At last.

***

Lewis sighs and puts down the phone. Another couple interested in Moor End Farm. Outsiders of course. No local wants to live there, only crazies from the cities who fancy a life far away from it all. They won't last long: if they buy it, which they probably will because of the price and the acreage, it will be a matter of months before they leave. Very few people can live with pounding on the windows in the dead of night, doors being flung open and shouts from the dark, windswept moors. Out they stumble into the pitch blackness: "Who's there? Who's there?"

Lewis twists the cheap, silver plated ring he wears on a chain around his neck. Forty years ago now. Forty years… Since Ruby died at the scene of that tragic accident. Since her family moved away to try and rebuild their lives. Since he went back to college and made a life for himself. And as his breath freezes on the suddenly icy air, he clasps the ring tightly. Ruby. She's here again.

13

MIDNIGHT CALLER

6am and bitterly cold. For most people the day would soon begin, but for those who had lain awake listening to his all-night radio show, the endlessness of grey dawn stretched ahead as usual. He called them his midnight people.

Leo pulled up his collar against the morning chill, footsteps echoing as he headed towards the neon-lit café on the corner. Open all night, the aroma of freshly percolated coffee and sizzling bacon drew in cabbies, shift workers and insomniacs alike.

Okay, so Ellen thought he was crazy - always heading straight home to bed herself after the show. But for Leo it was the best part of the day - staring through the steamy windows as hot, bitter espresso woke up his taste buds; watching the light chase shadows back under doors and into offices as the world of daylight people eased into life. Tired, pillow-creased faces stared unseeingly from bus windows at their own pale reflections, and council workers swept away the night's debris, preparing for a new day.

This had been his routine for nearly a year now and it suited him just fine.

"Great show last night, Leo."

Leo blinked, looked up and smiled at Dot, the café

proprietor. He held out his cup while she poured in more coffee. "Thanks."

"Shame that girl didn't phone last night."

"Natasha?"

Everyone was asking about Natasha. Even the local paper had got hold of the story and some of the midnight people were blogging about her too. Nothing like a real, live on-air romance for people to gossip about.

"That's the one." Dot gave him a saucy wink. "Got a thing for you, I'd say."

Leo forced another smile. As if anyone could possibly have a thing for him now - with his neck collar and more metal pins holding his limbs together than Bionic Man.

Besides, with Jenny gone, his heart had a hole in it the size of a crater. Nothing left to give.

Odd though, about Natasha. He'd kind of got used to her calling the show, his pulse picking up when he heard her voice.

At 7.45 am Leo paid his bill, folded up his newspaper, and made his way to the library. Today he would read about the big bang theory. Another day it might be child psychology. Anything. As long as it took his mind off his life and everything he'd hoped it would be before the accident. Before Jenny. Eventually he would drift home, like a ghost amongst the daylight people, to what he hoped would be a deep and dreamless sleep. But rarely was.

***

Midnight: Lights. Music. Action.

"Bet she calls tonight," said Ellen, putting on her headphones.

Leo could only raise his eyebrows in response, as the countdown for the show began: Three-two-one...

Automatically his voice dropped into a molasses-thick drawl that had earned him near cult status with his listeners. "Leo here for the Leo Logan show. Time to relax, kick off your shoes and listen to some great music…"

Lazy jazz oozed onto the airwaves as he took off his headphones. "I'll fetch some coffee."

"Actually I'll bet you ten pounds she calls tonight," said Ellen.

Leo affected shock. "What? Have I got 'Gullible' stamped across my forehead? No, make it something trickier - at least what she actually requests."

"Okay then - how about, 'Miss You Nights'?"

"Could be." That was certainly one of Natasha's favourites. "But I think It'll be, 'Help Me Make it Through the Night'." He tapped the side of his nose. "Call me psychic but that's the one she'll go with. And make it twenty."

"Ooh. Mr Confident."

Usually Natasha called in around 1am. If she hadn't called by 1.30am then generally speaking, she wasn't going to. It was 1.25am when Ellen took off her specs and rubbed the bridge of her nose. "Feeling a bit tired tonight," she said.

Leo wondered why she drove herself so hard. Like all the midnight people he guessed she had her reasons, and he suspected that like him, she couldn't sleep and when she did - the dreams came in a rush like the dark wall of a car crash.

"More of that lousy coffee?"

She nodded, managing a weary smile. Their eyes met and for a moment it looked as if she was about to say something. Leo waited. But then she bent her head to rummage for a tissue and the moment flew away.

At 1.32 am Natasha called the show. Static buzzed down the line.

"Hey, Natasha! How are you?"

After a couple of seconds Natasha said, "Hi Leo!"

He could almost hear the midnight people sigh with pleasure, fingers hovering over keyboards for the next instalment.

"Like to tell me what's keeping you awake tonight, Natasha?"

Natasha's voice was tiny and high like something Tinkerbell would have. She spoke all in a rush, "You know when there aren't any stars? When it's foggy and your house is surrounded by a thick blanket and you can't see? I get so scared sometimes."

"I know what you mean."

"I'm so alone."

"We're always here for you, Natasha."

"Do you feel lonely too, Leo?"

Leo hesitated. A line, he was sure, had been crossed. Something about the early hours made people confess secrets and dreams, but rarely did they make it personal with him in the way that Natasha did.

He sensed the listeners hold their collective breath and quickly decided not to bluff or try to lighten the mood. You always had to be careful with midnight people. "Yes," he said. "As a matter of fact I do."

Beside him Ellen stiffened.

"So, what can we play to chase away those shadows for you, Natasha? How about 'Help me Make it through …"

"That's cheating," Ellen mouthed furiously.

"'I Will Always Love You,'" said Natasha. "The Dolly

91

Parton version."

Leo looked at the two twenties he and Ellen had put on the desk and cringed inside. They had a broken-hearted girl here and the two of them had been taking bets.

"I think she's in love with you," Ellen sniffed, blowing her nose.

"No, I think she's just very, very lonely."

But crawling underneath his skin and lodging there was the thought that he was her lifeline - as if there was an invisible thread between them that she was holding on to.

***

"Natasha sounded sad last night," said Dot, putting a plate of bacon and eggs in front of him later that morning.

Leo grimaced. Just a hunch. But he too thought he'd detected a subtle change of mood, as if things might be coming to a head, or an end.

After a tormented, sleepless day, he took a stroll across the beach just as the sun was dropping like a flaming ball into the ocean. The sea hissed and shrank from the pebbles as darkness crept along the shore, lengthening his shadow. Along the coastline, lights flicked on and blinds were drawn. Soon it would be night again. Alone with the midnight people, prowling foxes and the belts of grey fog that rolled in from the sea.

Arriving at work early he was surprised to find Ellen, pink eyed and pale, already there. Why did she do this? Surely a young woman like her should be out partying, not working nights with an old cynic like himself? Well, he said old - he wasn't - he just felt as old as time. She'd evaded the topic when he'd asked her once, muttering something about it being her only way into radio. But Ellen never took holidays and to his knowledge there was no boyfriend, no 'Mr Ellen'.

"Actually I don't feel too good," she admitted.

"Why don't you go home?"

The producer was counting him in: "Three-two-one…"

Leo's voice immediately dipped into honey-coated dark chocolate, "It's midnight and you know what that means. It's the Leo Logan Show. Time to relax, unwind and enjoy…"

As Sade's silky tones began to croon, 'Smooth Operator,' over the airwaves, he noticed Ellen disappearing and unexpectedly his spirits plunged. Without her it would be a long night.

At 3 am Natasha called, catching him off guard.

"Hi Leo."

She started to tell him about swirling fog and hearing muffled voices. "I get so frightened. It's like I don't know where I am."

Leo struggled to understand, sensing her loneliness and wanting to help. Instead he asked her what music she'd like.

Static buzzed for a moment. Then she said, "You know that song - 'Did you happen to see the most beautiful girl in the world? And if you did…"

They both finished the lyrics together, "…Was she crying?"

"I know it," said Leo.

"Then go find her," said Natasha.

"What do you…?"

But the line was dead.

Go find her. Go find her… All night the words

reverberated in his head. Whatever had she meant by that? It just got stranger.

Next morning Dot was up to the toast and marmalade stage before she broached the subject. "What do you think she meant last night about go and find her?"

Leo shrugged. "I honestly don't know, Dot."

"I think she wants you to find out who she is."

He frowned. Natasha hadn't meant that. He was almost sure.

Ellen was off sick again the next night and the next. Nobody had heard from her and it hit Leo that he'd never asked, after nearly a year of working together, whether she lived alone. He soon found out that she did. By 6am he decided to find out if she was okay. And by 6.30 a sense of urgency gripped him.

When she answered the door to her flat wearing a pale pink dressing gown, her elfin face pinched and pale, something welled up from deep inside him and the urge to wrap her in his arms was overwhelming. *Go find her...Go find her...*This was it. His hollow heart flooded with warmth.

"I heard what she said the other night," Ellen croaked as she snuggled against his chest. "Do you think she meant me?" Their glances met and both smiled shyly as the early morning sun slanted through the blinds. And a new day began.

***

Natasha never called the station again, a fact remarked upon and discussed by many. A heated local debate followed. The press pushed for a campaign to find Natasha and then, as quickly as the issue arose it was dropped.

Night after night, Leo and Ellen sat listening to the

debate, hands held tightly.

The blinking emergence into the world of daylight people had not been easy for either of them, disquiet mellowing only with time, ghosts receding gradually and gracefully into the shadows. Moving into the glare of the sun took courage and each other, the pace of life faster, the noises sharper. Eventually Leo resumed his position at the local paper where he had worked with Jenny; and Ellen found part time work as an assistant producer with the radio station.

A year later they married. A quiet ceremony at a church near the beach. An ancient creaking building that rattled with ocean breezes and dozed to the crash of pounding surf. The day was bright and clear with scudding clouds chasing sunshine over the hills. And later, hours and hours away, after a bouncing flight through the velvet night, they arrived at a tiny Caribbean island.

Exhausted, they slept with the patio doors open, lying deeply and dreamlessly, content, still holding hands.

At 1.27 am precisely the phone rang.

Automatically Leo stretched out an arm.

Static. And then a tiny Tinkerbell voice squeaked excitedly, "It's Natasha. I'm through the fog. I found what I had to do so you could live again. And now I'm free. We both are."

Suddenly he remembered - *Natasha! It was Jenny's favourite name.*

"There's so much light here."

He struggled to understand. "Light? Where?"

"Good-bye, Leo. Be happy."

"No, don't go...Jenny..."

As soon as Ellen woke he related what had happened,

but she started shaking her head. "No, Leo - it must have been a dream."

"But don't you see? She loved the name," Leo insisted. "It all makes sense! Jenny always said if she'd been called something like Natasha her life would have been different - more exotic. That was no dream - it was Jenny."

Ellen leaned over and kissed him gently. "I believe you, Leo. But look!"

She was staring at the conch by the side of the bed - this was a tiny island retreat. With no phone lines.

14

ISLANDS

The plane is heavy, dropping its night-weary cargo through rising coils of steam. She braves a glance out of the window at the islands below, sprawling like spores in a petri dish, and wonders where or how they will land. A brilliant Eastern sun flashes across the cabin, heat scorching the glass as they sink through the ether. Fin squeezes her hand. This is their new life, not a honeymoon, but years and years. There was no choice. It was either this or lose him. No choice, no choice - she tells herself over and over - what else could she have done?

***

Waiting in Arrivals is Katya. She welcomes Fin with smiling enthusiasm, blue-black hair bouncing silkily on china doll shoulders; cold, pale fingers limply brushing Lily's outstretched hand. Strutting ahead, Katya directs the couple to a waiting company car and Lily, noting her thin bowed legs - chicken legs - permits herself a small smile until she catches her own reflection. God, how enormous! How pink, blotchy, creased and frizzy and…she is unprepared for the oven door blast of heat as they are rushed from air-conditioned efficiency into equatorial humidity, and the first trickle of sweat worming down her back.

Singapore: the city, the island. Fin is delivered to a

tower of reflective glass and Lily to a hotel, with the cases. A doorman dressed entirely in white looks through her with dead eyes. She is used to being looked at by men but these men don't see her - small and neat, they hurry past shouting staccato English into mobiles, or stare blankly from guard positions with guns tucked into holsters. She smiles tentatively, politely passing the time of day until the heat wrings her dry and exhausted - catapulted through days as fast as the dainty women with sharp, glossy ebony hair who click-clack past in black Chanel.

Eventually she settles on an apartment: high-rise and not what she had in mind, but the rents are thousands of dollars a week and Katya is showing impatience. Five days now and the temperature is rising - an omnipotent soup of baking heat that seethes with screeching cicadas. Lily turns up the air-con and lies spread-eagled on the double bed, fair hair plastered to clammy skin. Years and years, she's thinking, years and years...

The weeks roll like a heavy nimbostratus into December. Tinsel, strung from lampposts, sizzles in the midday sun and the smell of frying sesame oil cloys the air. It is a relief to dive into an air-conditioned shopping mall, rather like being, she thinks, a freshly boiled ham popped into the fridge. She is hoping to find something larger than a size six amongst the bright, candy coloured clothes. Something suitable because all she has is shorts and this sets her apart, placing her firmly in the bulging tourist category. Seizing a black shift dress she takes it to the assistant. A size twelve perhaps? A pair of shark eyes meets hers. "Extra-large," is shrieked across the shop floor. "No, nothing in extra-large, ma'am."

She turns to hide her sweeping embarrassment,

leafing through tiny Lycra dresses not big enough to fit a child.

A girl appears at her elbow with a calculator. "I do you special deal - four for three."

"No, no thanks."

"Okay - four for two, un?"

She shakes her head. "No, really. No."

Once more she plunges into the throng of Orchard Road and the furnace blasts her skin. But now there is a subtle alteration in the light, making everything seem extra vivid, almost surreal, and a wind has picked up; at first playing with, then thrashing the palm trees. Rapidly the street clears and the ever-present drilling, and whirring of cranes, stops. Lights flick on. Silence precedes a long, low whistle. And then it strikes: two, three, four… forks of white lightning streak through the sky with a deafening crack that rattles windows and shakes foundations.

Lily lifts her face to splashes of cold rain until she's blinking and gasping, goose pimples chasing up and down her bare arms; soaked in an instant, drenched by a stampede of rain that drills pavements and hammers roads, bouncing off car bonnets, swirling in torrents of gushing, brown water that cascades into drains.

When it stops, minutes later, steam shimmies off the surfaces like a Turkish sauna. Cars reappear. Cafés empty out. And life continues as before.

She wants to tell Fin how the water sloshed warm around her ankles, how the lightning ripped through the sky, how she walked through steam with her clothes pasted to her skin. But he doesn't come home. So she lies on the bed while the air-con hums and daylight drops abruptly into night, her sodden sandals and ruined dress flung where she left them - on the tiled floor with her muddy footprints.

They are in a restaurant, jostling elbows with Singaporeans flicking rice into their mouths from tiny bowls, when Fin says, "It's the Christmas party tomorrow night."

Lily stirs the dish of broccoli that was carelessly plonked in front of her, having requested the vegetarian option. The broccoli is still hard and the water copious. "Where are they taking us?"

"Ah." Fin dabs his mouth. He doesn't mind playing roulette with what he orders from an indecipherable menu, swallows what he thinks was a tiny foot. "I'm afraid wives aren't invited. Katya says…"

"Katya says!" Lily raises her voice, slams down the chopstick she has been using to catch a floret. "Katya says this and Katya says that! What about me? It's Christmas for God's sake!"

"I know, I know. I'm sorry, babe."

Lily's stomach growls loudly and a boiling temper threatens to erupt. She pushes the steaming bowl away. "I don't think I can do this, Fin. I've tried but I really hate it here." Now she has said the word, 'hate' out loud it somehow fuels her rage. She looks at him and she hates him too - with his floppy hair and weak chin. She barely knows him. "I'm hungry, I'm boiling hot and I'm bored, lonely, homesick…" The list is long and she tails off as his attention begins to wander around the room.

Eventually he says, sucking up his last noodle. "Why don't you join a club? An ex-pat wives club? All the others do."

She hasn't envisaged herself like this before: an ex-pat wife. She mulls it over. Pictures tea and scones, lounging on verandas overlooking pools or tea plantations, laughing with other women wearing big, white hats. She nods. Okay, yeah, okay - she'll try it.

***

Woks

She chooses a group, which does not involve breast-feeding or toddlers. This club is led by a Texan called Sherry who calls it 'Woks' - Women without Kids. "Why doncha come and see me, honey?" says Sherry. "I'm on my lonesome right now, wrapping presents for the folks comin' over."

This is too quick for Lily, who arranges instead to meet the following morning at the Shangri-La Hotel, where she will be introduced to the other 'girls' - Dulcie from Idaho and Marcia from Essex.

When she walks in wearing a sleeveless, cotton sundress she finds Dulcie bursting out of a red business suit, rings flashing on every manicured finger. Dulcie's hair is a backcombed bouffant of mahogany, her nails long and red. When she smiles the heavy foundation folds into creases and movie-star teeth are bared. Marcia, too, leaps forward, heavy in a turquoise velour tracksuit and matching turban. Her plump feet are squeezed into gold pumps, which curl up at the toes like mini gondolas.

Sherry holds court. "You must come to one of our little lunches."

Marcia looks Lily up and down. "It's five hundred dollars a head but well worth it," she says. "We go once a week, don't we girls?"

Noting Lily's widening eyes, Sherry's wide smile fades a fraction. "This is a club. We do stuff, you know? Johor, Java, Bangkok - something each week. You wanna join?"

Lily nods. Sod the money - she'll find it.

"What's hubby do?" says Sherry.

"Oh, erm - banking."

"Know Al Baker?"

"Um…"

"You gotta know people, sweetie. This is a real, small place." Sherry calls for tea and cakes. "We always get cakes."

Dulcie leans close. "This is such a great place to pick up men, don't you find?"

Close up, Dulcie's skin is like rhino hide, her hooded eyes reptilian beneath azure powder and false eyelashes. Lily mutters something about being newly married and the women roll their eyes.

"Goddammitt!" Dulcie shrieks. "Oh no. I've got a broken toe nail."

Lily starts to laugh but the other two dive towards Dulcie's offending foot and Sherry puts an arm around her friend. "Don't worry, honey. It will soon grow back."

Later, much later - weeks or months - the days have blurred in a myriad of afternoon teas with champagne, plane hops for shopping by day, bars by night, the women besieged by dusky barefoot children pleading, "Buy, you buy, Lady - you buy?" Every day hot and wet or hot and steamy or hot and sunny. But there is a problem at the bank. "Whadya mean you can't come?" Sherry snaps on the phone. "The ticket's bought."

Lily's cards are maxed out and the monthly allowance Fin gives her barely covers the minimum repayments. She has no cash.

"Forget it," says Sherry, and Lily can hear her popping gum. "Have this one on me."

"Oh no I couldn't possibly…"

But the line is dead.

They're going to Johor on another shopping trip. It has become impossible to say no, to say to women whose husbands own global companies that she's hocked to the eyeballs in debt. Debt. She says the word out loud and lets it hang in the tiled apartment, wafting on the air-con. What the hell has she gone and done? A tiny knot ties itself into the top corner of her stomach and lodges there. Could she tell Fin? That floppy haired guy who took her out and told her he loved her - a lifetime away when she was a different person, a girl waiting on tables, wondering what to do with her life - who was he? A boyish smile and a knack of making her laugh and she'd followed him to the other side of the world.

***

Lying on her bed she stares out at a sea of high-rise apartments and cranes, silent now, picked out like dinosaurs against the bruised night sky. Somewhere in the block a pneumatic drill finally stops, leaving a humming space in her consciousness, and a door slams. She's drowsy but thoughts are bubbling to the surface: more money and she could spend her days without thinking, wondering where Fin was and why he'd brought her here. Had it looked better for his career if he was married? An image of his grinning freckle-face dangles before her and fingers of fury begin to crawl underneath her skin. Oh the humiliation - to have thought it was love when all he'd done was choose an accessory as coolly as selecting a briefcase!

Home then. She sits up, eyes wide. Home. Solution. Yes, of course. Fly home. The prospect of taking a backwards step is at first unappealing: she pictures her parents' thirties semi in Whitstable, the clock ticking methodically on the mantelpiece, the bottle-green sofa, the ornaments dusted daily. Of her old bedroom with its pink walls and posters of pop groups long consigned to rehab clinics and divorce courts. Tick-tock, tick-tock, whatever would she do?

But there is the lure of snuggling into a winter coat, curling up in an armchair by the fire with a good book, ducking into an old pub that hums with neighbourly chat and oh, heaven, the crisp, frosty morning air… and every little thing that she ever took for granted.

She sees now why they call missing home a sickness. Suddenly there's a family holiday in Bude, her father's battered old Fiesta parked over the bay, she and her mother reading paperbacks while the Atlantic hurls pebbles onto the beach and sleet spatters the windscreen. There is the little envelope arriving each week at college, just a few pounds her mother sends. The rushed wedding with no photographer, her mum and dad lost among the champagne fuelled bankers who came to the pub afterwards.

How cheaply she has sold herself.

And now she has no money. Worse, she owes money. Thousands. She questions again if she can tell Fin, contemplates how he will react and realises she doesn't know. Lily flops back and closes her eyes, making no attempt to blink away the salty tears running into her hair. What will she do? Whatever will she do?

***

When tomorrow comes it is Johor, where men lurk in bars and ride dirt bikes up and down the street. They call out, "Hey, Lady!"

A hop across the causeway in Dulcie's red Mercedes -

Johor is full of forbidden things like cigarettes and gum and litter and spitting. Lily tags behind Sherry and the girls as they stroll around markets tasting food and haggling over sarongs, enjoying the attention of dark-eyed men lurking in alleyways, their own women covered and veiled, minding children.

Lily walks into a bar, eyed from the gloom like bats in a cave. She orders a beer and then another until a golden skinned boy slides onto the stool next to her. He passes her a cigarette from his shirt pocket and she surprises herself by taking it, thinking 'what the hell?' when he asks her why she's looking sad. So she tells him and he makes a call. "I can help you."

Lily shrugs.

Sherry, Dulcie and Marcia will be in a hotel by now drinking champagne. Her world and theirs: the two have touched, theirs sliding over hers like mist on a swamp. Her new friend snaps shut his mobile phone and it seems to her, right there and then, as she sits drinking on the edge of sanity, that dipping into a much darker one is the only way out.

***

Christmas

Christmas Eve and she spends it alone wandering around another faceless shopping mall. *Rudolph the red-nosed reindeer, had a very shiny nose...* On the top tier she looks over and wonders how it might feel to throw herself off with limbs outstretched, onto the enormous, shimmering chandelier below. Would anyone notice? Might she hang there for days, gently grilling on the elegant crystal?

On Christmas Day they eat a Christmas Dinner Lily has sweated over in the kitchen. With windows open she can hear the woman next door shouting continuously, "wah, wah, ho, ha, un?" And the replies, "wah, wah, un?"

Afterwards Fin opens the local paper. "Druggies caught," he says absent-mindedly. "We'll not hear anything more about them, that's for sure - curtains for the poor buggers. They shoot them here, you know. Shoot them in the head. That's it, no nonsense."

Lily's stomach clenches so hard it threatens to expunge everything she's eaten. Acid burns in her throat and for a second blackness engulfs her. "Shoot them? What do you mean, shoot them? They can't do that."

Fin looks at her as if seeing her for the first time. "My God, you really are naïve aren't you?"

She thinks about the armed guards who follow her round department stores, remembers Fin laughing about how he left the keys in his Audi all night. Those Malay boys on bikes, little packages and big money. It had been easy. At twenty-three she looked like a daughter on a shopping trip with her mother, had been waved impatiently through from Johor by unsmiling officials. Just another daytrip. One more time and she could go home, light as air. Just one more.

But now anger sparks as she recalls the dirty bar, the taut, smooth-skinned boy with a cigarette balancing on his lower lip, the ready cash. How careless with her life. Her life! And he knew. She couldn't even bank it. Jesus - she'd been going to do that this week.

"You okay?" He no longer calls her babe she notices.

"Yeah." Look, she got away with it. No more trips and she'd be fine. Except for the cash. Rolls and rolls of it. She starts to speak, saying the first thing, anything - "We should talk, Fin. How's work going?"

"What do you mean?"

"I mean - you're always there. You must be doing well?"

He shrugs, keeps his eyes on the newspaper. "Yes."

"When you work late, where are you? Restaurants with clients? What?" *With Katya?*

Fin looks up. "What is this? Twenty questions? I work hard, okay? You know the business I'm in - I have to catch the London and New York markets. End of."

His mouth is sealed tightly and Lily finds she can't look at him for a moment longer. There he sits casually leafing through the paper when he's ruined her life.

She stares out of the window overlooking the pool, at the silky palm trees and the stick man brushing away leaves, shuffling round the edge with a broom, pretending not to look at the glistening flesh of ex-pat women displayed in bikinis. *Two worlds touching…*

"Why don't we go to Sentosa tomorrow?" Fin asks, forcing a smile. "A proper day out."

She jumps visibly. "Sentosa? Why? Why there?"

"I just think it would get us out."

***

Sentosa

The day is stormy and the wind whips across the island, rocking the cable cars. They are high up, about half way across to Sentosa when a jagged fork of lightning flashes vertically overhead, the sky ominously dark. Work has stopped and the crane lights are on. For a moment there is nothing but the sound of whirring and creaking. Then a deafening crack. The cable car vibrates alarmingly. Screams from other cars. Fin reaches for her hand. Slowly they buzz forward towards Sentosa. "Don't look back," he says.

She can't help it. Her neck creaks round on its stem. More forks - three, then four...six, seven - malicious, pointed fingers striking randomly at skyscrapers, hotels and ships. Explosions tear through the sky as slowly they drift over the ocean, rocking precariously in their glass bubble, a deep, grey fog rolling behind as if to swallow them whole. Sentosa is now in sight. Ahead is an exotic bird sanctuary.

"We should head for that," he says, grabbing her arm as they jump free and start to run. A violent gust flattens the palm trees and sea spray stings their faces. Great spots of rain land as puddles, jumping off the path, pounding their heads until they can barely see.

Then abruptly, as they level with the birdhouse, it stops. There is a biblical shaft of light and a hot sun prises back the clouds. "I've got something to tell you," Fin says. "And you're going to have to be brave."

The birds are squawking so loudly she can hardly hear.

"Keep walking," he says. "And don't scream or shout or anything."

"Fin! What - what do you mean, scream?" The knot in her stomach is growing, her heart banging hard in her chest, ears, head, eyes. He knows, he must know. He's found all those wads of dollars rolled up in the wardrobe, stuffed into handbags, and now he's going to say something terrible, something she can't cope with. A women's prison - a lawyer he knows, the British Embassy. She can scarcely breathe.

They pause outside the orioles' cage. A parrot screeches,'so cute, so cute...'

Fin hangs his head, floppy hair no longer endearing but irritating. She wishes he would get it cut. "What is it?

What?"

"We've got to leave. Look, I know you love it here now with your friends but We've got to leave…"

Lily stares at this man. He thinks she's happy. He actually thinks she is happy. He's saying things about mistakes, investing in collapsing markets, shifting funds, and she struggles to understand.

"What are you talking about?"

His expression contorts into one of exasperated contempt. "Aren't you listening? It's going to hit the fan, Lily. Big time. We have to go tomorrow night."

She stares and stares. He thinks she's happy. He's been doing things that put them in jeopardy and he never talked to her. And yet… "We have to leave," he'd said. Leave. Oh God, she thinks, thank you.

***

The plane thunders down the runway, lights flashing, trolleys and overhead lockers rattling furiously. This time she and Fin are quiet - no champagne, no kisses, shackled into economy class, heads low. As the jet lifts off, banking sharply to the left, she leans against the window, staring into the velvet night at islands becoming smaller and smaller until they are little more than placemats of orange lights on huge black tables. Somewhere, someone rummaging through dustbins on a back street in Chinatown, is going to get lucky. Win the lottery without a ticket.

Lily closes her eyes. They'll be waiting for Fin, probably. And for her - life will pick up where it was before - tougher now, and alone. But she has her life. And she's going home.

15

ELEANOR

Today Eleanor is moving out. She drops her two nightdresses, a pair of faded slippers and a wash bag into a scuffed, pink suitcase the size of a child's.

"Come along, Ellie," says the big, florid woman who smells of nicotine, sweat and crisps. "The taxi will be here soon."

Eleanor stares at Brenda with round, empty eyes as she rocks from one foot to the other before crumpling onto the bed, pulling repeatedly at her hair. *It won't be for long - you must do as you're told - We'll come and see you, of course we will....*

Brenda sighs. "Whatever's the matter now? I would have thought you'd be dying to get out of this flamin' mausoleum. They're knocking it down, love, and not before time. You're going to a bright new place with your own bedroom and a kitchen. You'll love it. Freedom, Ellie - just think!"

Eleanor thinks of the ones she will be living with. Of skinny, black-eyed Carol who darts like a fugitive, hiding behind cupboards, screaming and shaking her fists at the radio. She pictures Edith with her frizzy mass of grey hair and huge, bulging belly, who says she ate a snake. Tiny, birdlike Dot who chatters to herself incessantly in a language all her own. And Vera. Vera with a habit of smacking whoever she walks past - usually so violently they're knocked flat to the wall. Eleanor starts to cry.

Brenda sighs again, loudly, and begins to stuff Eleanor's belongings into the pink case: an ancient, ragged teddy bear, a chenille dressing gown, support tights and underwear over-washed to grey.

"It should be me what's crying, Eleanor. Me! It's me what's losing my job - you're going to get care in the community, love."

A mini-bus draws up outside and Eleanor watches from the window as a bald man in a bright orange jacket jumps out whistling. He swings open the back doors and a cluster of elderly people shuffle towards him, some unsure, some beginning to elbow themselves to the front.

"Come on, darlin'," he shouts jovially, taking one of the old ladies by the arm. "Mind how you go, sweetheart."

One of the group wanders off - Eleanor recognises the tiny, hunched figure of Dot in her lilac cardigan and pink fluffy slippers, heading for the middle of the lawn, chattering urgently to herself. The man reclaims her, manoeuvring his charge into the van. Soon it will be Eleanor's turn. She should be down there, case packed, eager for a new life. Except this has been her home now for nearly seventy years. She is the shadow of a life not lived, a face at the window peering through bars with haunted eyes, waiting for the dinner bell.

She wonders what she should do - her head is empty and silent - and tears drip down her quilted, tissue cheeks while her neck jerks uncomfortably. She used to mind when her face muscles jumped around like a badly behaved marionette, but she is used to it now, to how her tongue flicks out like an iguana snatching lunch, to how her legs jitter. To looking like a lunatic.

"Well that's it," says Brenda. "All packed. Come on now, love."

Eleanor stays rooted to the bed.

"Now, Eleanor!"

She dips her head, bites her lip, eyes darting furtively from left to right.

Brenda sighs again, hauling Eleanor to her feet with one quick, well-practised lunge. With the pink suitcase on her arm, she clasps Eleanor's small, papery white hand and drags her from the dormitory.

The corridors are empty, tiled in bottle green with mosaic floors smooth from decades of shuffling feet. Eleanor hangs heavily behind Brenda, delaying the journey towards the sunlit reception area - the wood panelled, red-carpeted entrance with its portraits of Victorian patrons staring from hooded eyes, their tiny rosebud mouths holy and censorious.

Eleanor whimpers, "Where's Mother? I want to see Mother."

"She passed on, love," says Brenda.

"She said she'd come back."

"She's been dead this past twenty years, love."

Eleanor's eyes widen as she digests the information. Her mouth tightens. A scream erupts. Screaming, screaming, screaming. Hands fastening onto hers. Shouts. Sinking into blackness.

***

The new home does not smell clean for long. Edith has peed on the grey cord sofa and Dot has hidden a stash of mouldy cakes under her bed. Stale clothes are dumped in white, chipboard drawers on top of clean ones, and Vera discovers a cutlery drawer.

Eleanor, muzzy-headed, sits on her bed and begins to thread the sheets through agitated fingers. Her case is still in the hallway and it is ten past one - lunch is half an hour late and there is no smell of cooking. What will happen? Who will make the meal?

High-pitched shrieks emanate from the room next door. Dot comes over to Eleanor's bed and stands over her, discussing something urgently in her strange secret language, eyes flashing black as a bird's. Someone is shouting - Carol has been attacked with a fork and Vera taken away.

It is dark before Eleanor is found curled up on her bed - a tight ball with claw hands, and clumps of hair strewn across the pillow.

"Eleanor?" The voice is calm, soothing.

Eleanor opens her eyes but does not turn.

"Have you been taking your tablets?"

She stares at the new person leaning over her. Close cropped hair. A long, fine nose. Piercing blue eyes.

"Are you feeling all right?"

Eleanor starts to cry. "I've just lost my mother."

"I don't think you've taken your tablets, have you? Remember what we said about that? I'm going to need to give you a little injection, okay?"

She feels nothing. And when she wakes, the ceiling seems very far away, as if the distance between herself and the rest of the world has elongated in a hall of mirrors. A face looms over her, then fades, with a little quiver of adjustment, like a ghost into the scenery. A door bangs, someone is moaning quietly, disinfectant assaults her nostrils, and then it is dark. *Good.*

Back in her customary haze, the terror relinquishes its hallucinatory grip. Fingers of an early grey dawn creep around the curtains and trucks trundle past the window. She wanders over to see. There's a shout from a drunk staggering up the street, waving a bottle. A car radio: '*Her name is Rio and she dances on the sand...*' The smell of fried food and petrol wafts through on a wave of neon mist.

She marvels at the window being left ajar - and breathes in deeply. She was a girl, a child, and now she is...Eleanor frowns...what happened in the middle?

A therapist is coming, says the young girl leading her back to the bed. Eleanor is cold now, skin marbled, shivering. "I've unpacked your things and there's some tea and toast if you want some?"

The young woman seems kind and Eleanor smiles tentatively, allowing herself to be led to the bathroom, undressed and helped to wash. "Takes some getting used to, this looking after yourself malarkey after all those years, I suppose?"

Eleanor stares at her, letting the woman dry in between her toes, then roll a sweater over her head. The hands that brush against her are small and feathery light, quite different from Brenda's impatient, bundling spades. For now her tics are still and her head is clear. Somehow voices seem louder and colours brighter. She starts at the sound of a lorry rumbling past.

The girl's eyes are round and hazel. "Are you okay?"

Eleanor stares like a hibernating animal emerging from its lair. The bathroom smells sweetly of pears and coconuts. It is warm and steamy and there are towels of pink and yellow piled up on racks. In the mirror the face looking back is ravaged - dark, hollow eyes set in lavender bruises, sallow skin clinging to jutting cheekbones, and wisps of white hair sprouting from a shiny scalp.

"You're getting a therapist today. Did you remember?"

Eleanor frowns. They said in a week. Has a week gone by?

"Her name's Christine. She's quite nice."

***

Christine wears jeans, a poncho, and lots of coloured beads. She jangles with bracelets and earrings. Refers to Eleanor as her client. It would be lovely, says Christine, if Eleanor were to open up about her past.

"Tell me," she says, over mugs of instant coffee. "Tell me what you remember, poppet."

Eleanor, whose mind has cleared in recent days, tries to stop her legs from juddering violently.

"When did you first start taking the anti-psychotics? Can you remember?"

Eleanor's face begins to twitch again.

"Okay." Christine takes a sip of coffee and dips in a digestive. "According to the notes - you're self-medicating. How are you coping with that?"

Eleanor thinks about the tablets in the packet she has in her bedside cabinet. "The blue ones?"

"Yes. Are you taking them?"

She shakes her head. "Um…"

"You see - this is where it all goes wrong. I want you to come off them, my love. Since They've knocked down that Victorian mausoleum you were in, We've unearthed all the old records. You were never mentally ill. Did you know that?"

Eleanor starts to rock back and forth, to wring her hands.

"Apparently you had a child with a man your parents didn't think suitable and you didn't want to give up the child. They thought a short stint of cold baths and electric shock treatment would make you come to your senses. Honestly, it just defies belief!" Christine's voice has risen by at least an octave.

"Mother is coming back, isn't she?" Eleanor begins to whimper.

"What? No, of course not."

"But she promised." Eleanor stares into a far corner of the room, her voice high-pitched and child-like. "I remember that doctor - the one with the black hairs on the back of his hands. Like spiders' legs. He said it wouldn't be for long."

"Eleanor, please sit down."

But Eleanor begins to cry. A whimper at first. And then a scream. She picks up her mug and hurls it at the wall, runs into the bedroom and tears sheets from the beds. "She said she'd come back. Where is she? My mother!"

Now there are people holding her. A needle stinging her thigh.

And she is fifteen again. Turning her face to the wall, while outside sunlight dapples the manicured lawns through swaying oaks, and inside the aroma of over-boiled vegetables wafts down the hospital corridors.

It won't be for long - chin up, old girl. We'll come and see you when the war's over - make a fresh start.

Blackness. Nothing. Bliss…

16
RETRIBUTION

The cell was sparse - just a table with two chairs positioned at opposite sides - and I was cold and fed up. "I can't explain. I don't know."

His hard, black stare bore right through me. "Try."

"You won't believe me. You'll think I'm making it all up so what's the use?"

"Try me."

"It's Karen, she's mad."

He raised a caterpillar eyebrow, his voice shot through with steel. "Start from the beginning, Lily. This is extremely serious. You do understand what a mess you're in, don't you?"

I nodded mutely as my stomach tumbled like a washing machine. When was it I had last eaten? Probably days ago. Certainly it felt like days. Or maybe hours. Without a window or clock I'd lost all track of time, but one thing I did know - there was no way I was getting out if I didn't talk. I sighed heavily, shoulders slumped, picking at my nails. "Okay. Well we met on the training course about three months ago."

"Who?"

"Me and Karen. Well, Tamsin was on the course too but it was Karen I hit it off with. Right away we were like, so close. She'd only have to look at me and I knew what she was thinking. Worrying really, now I know how mad she is. I mean - what does that say about me? "

I laughed.

He didn't. "Go on."

"We really liked each other, that's all - found the same things funny. We had to sit through these God-awful training seminars from boring, pumped up pin-heads in suits. She'd say something like, "I want to club him to death with my umbrella," and I'd be doubled up because she had long, curly red hair and an umbrella with Pink Panther on it. So funny…"

I looked into his impassive bulldog face and reckoned he'd had the old humour bypass. Still, in light of the situation… "No, okay, not nice. But funny. Yeah - funny. And like I said, I didn't know… I just got sort of sucked in. Look, it gets a bit tricky from here. Could I like, have a cup of tea or something?"

"No."

"Okay then." Jeez, my mouth was dry and what was coming up was going to make me sound like a freaking lunatic. "Right well I'll just get it over with and you can think what you like, but I swear on my mother's life it's the truth, okay?"

"I hope you get on with your mother, Lily, because it had better be."

"Yeah." I looked at him through strands of greasy hair. I felt awful, needed a shower. By then I just wanted to get out of there. "Well, this other girl, Tamsin Lewis, she really got on our nerves. I mean, she really, really grated. She was like, oh you know the type - short, tight skirts, always bending over and making doe eyes at the men. She did my head in. Right tart. If she had to stand up and do a presentation she'd be like sticking out her chest and tossing her hair about, eye-to-eye with Phil - he's our boss - and ignoring everyone else. Of course we found out later the two of them were at it…"

"At what?"

I squirmed. "*It.* We'd be staying away at a hotel, the whole team, and he'd be like, carrying her bags for her. I did, we did, you know - really hate her. And then once the course was over she got these amazing sales results when we knew she was a hopeless slag, and we had degrees and she didn't."

"And is that when you and Karen decided to teach her a lesson?"

"No. We didn't know how bad it was at that point. It was about a month later when the bonus payments came out and she got £1500 while we got nothing. I mean - imagine - you're earning £12000 a year and you've got nothing left at the end of the month after tax and mortgage and bills. A quarterly bonus of £1500! Well that's a lot, mate." I could feel my face getting hot and that pressure cooker feeling inside again. Even after our revenge I was still incensed at the unfairness. The sheer injustice of what happened.

The man with the black eyes sat and waited. He was getting what he wanted. He knew it was coming - I could read him and I wanted to hold back but I couldn't. Like a volcano lain dormant the eruption had started and it wouldn't stop.

"Anyway, that's when she made her mistake. Tamsin. She told, and this is how stupid she is, she actually told Karen in a drunken bragging session in the bar that Phil had done her sales negotiations for her. Can you believe that? For a shag with that tart he sold *our* supplies into *her* wholesalers so *she* got the credit. So there Karen and I were - selling, selling, selling to all these shops and all the time they were buying from Tamsin's wholesalers because she had the better price. The whole thing stank." By then my fingers where clawing into my palms and my mouth felt so tight I was surprised the words could spit themselves out.

"And that was when…"

"That was when it started, yes."

And oh boy did it start. As soon as Karen found out what was going on she motioned for me to drink up. We were going back to her place. She drove in total silence, chain smoking and gripping the wheel with hands like white claws. When we screeched into her driveway, she slammed the door shut so hard the car bounced.

"Listen, Lily," she said, the second we were in through the front door. "We have to do something about that whinging little bitch."

A bottle of vodka later we were cackling away, pure venom pulsing through our arteries. No point going to Phil. He was the boss and to him sex spoke louder than anything we had to say on injustice.

"I'm going down the pan," Karen said, waving her cigarette around. "Flushed down the bog on a credit card."

"Me too."

"While Tamsin turns up dressed in cashmere and Karen Millen I can't even afford a splurge at Florence and Fred. No holiday this year either."

I thought of the week I'd hoped to have in the Grand Canaries and knew I'd be painting the spare bedroom instead. That £1500 would have paid off my card and bought me a week on a beach somewhere. "What shall we do? I mean it can't go on, can it?"

Karen broke into another bottle and passed me the fag packet. "Retribution."

"How?"

"Come with me."

I should have stopped then but every time I paused for breath I saw Tamsin's simpering smile. Heard her whiny voice telling Phil how she was 'going to go all the way' and when he smirked and glanced at the others in the team with a knowing look, she'd look all faux-innocent like she didn't know what she'd said.

"So there we were."

The man with the black eyes stared at me unblinkingly. "Sitting in front of Karen's computer?"

I nodded.

"Be very careful now, Lily. You must tell me precisely what happened next. Leave nothing out."

"Okay. Well we were four sheets to the wind by then. And Karen had some pills she said were just herbal but I didn't care - I chucked one down my throat anyway with another shot of vodka on top. And then we were on this site. We typed in 'revenge'."

I screwed up my face trying hard to remember. We'd both drawn breath when we saw it - a bright orange, fiery background and black capital letters with 'Ultimate Retribution' written across it. We clicked to enter the site and selected 'Injustice.' There were 7 easy steps, it said, to initiate universal retribution. The cosmic laws of injustice must always balance, and it was our duty to right the wrong. Just 7 easy steps and Tamsin would get her comeuppance. We loved it.

"Then once we were in we had to agree to the 7 steps, which we did. Step 1 - that was easy. Logging in and signing up. Karen logged in as Cruella and I was

Boudicca. So funny. Then we typed in our details and moved onto Step 2. That was where we put in Tamsin's details - name, address, mobile, car registration, physical description. Actually it was quite comprehensive but we didn't care - we wanted someone to sort her out."

"Eliminate her?"

I squirmed again at that. "Well…maybe just a good kicking."

"So you weren't clear?"

"Oh we were at the time. We wanted her dead and buried but of course we were drunk and high and…"

"And you're making excuses."

"Yes. No. Look, I'm just saying how it was, okay? After that we had to select the level of punishment required so we selected Death. Is that clear enough for you?"

"You definitely selected Death?"

"Yes. Frankly we figured she deserved everything she got. Anyway, after that it was onto Level 4. This was where we would be contacted by email and texts: when we received a question we must answer 'yes' or there would be negative consequences. We were asked if we understood and we clicked on 'yes.' Then we were asked again and we had to click 'yes' again. It was very exciting. Can't remember how I got home. Must have slept on Karen's floor."

The next day was a bit of a blur. It was a weekday and I was driving along a dual carriageway when my carphone bleeped and I picked up a text. When I pulled over it was 'Darth Veda' asking me if they should go ahead. Vaguely flashing back to the emphatic order to always say 'yes' when asked a question I texted back affirmative. This then happened several more times and again by email when I logged on that evening. I remember texting Karen to ask her if she had also had these questions, and she texted back a stupid smiley face and I laughed. I couldn't remember much from the night before except we'd been on this weird website and it was all...well...adrenalin pumping, I suppose.

"Then some time during the night I got another text telling me I would start to see signs in the media - to look out for coded messages about Tamsin, that the Cosmos now knew she must be eliminated and that it was up to me to do it. I have to say that scared me a bit. I was thinking that maybe Karen was a mad person. Like in a horror movie - you know?"

"And did you receive these coded messages?"

"Yes."

"And then what? Level 5?"

"I got an email the following day saying I had passed Level 4 and now the Cosmos would exact retribution on Tamsin Lewis. I had to log on to the site again and sign in. I would then be able to choose the method of her destruction. At the time I was putting in my sales for the day and the whole thing was freaking me out so I didn't do it. I thought the best thing would be for me to get another job or something. Walk away - you know..."

"Only you weren't allowed to."

"No. I got a coded message to tell me that I had signed a contract and must complete the course of action or the consequences to myself would come back a hundred fold."

The man nodded solemnly. "Go on."

I remember waking at six the next morning with a thudding heart. I hadn't logged on and now something awful would happen to me. I managed to shrug off the feeling and shower, dress, have breakfast, but there was a sales meeting that morning and I was cloaked in this overpowering feeling of doom.

The first person I saw was a happy, smiling Tamsin showing off her engagement ring. A junior doctor whose parents were buying them both a house as a wedding present. Karen and I exchanged glances loaded with genetically coded emotions: obviously the poor guy didn't know she was screwing her married boss. Just a convenient little hobby eh, Tamsin? An arrangement that suited.

Phil then decided we should have a little quiz as a warm-up. The prize would be a Smart phone. Tamsin won it. Swiftly afterwards Karen and I met in the toilets.

"Tamsin knew the answers," Karen hissed as we washed our hands. "She and Phil met an hour early to 'go over her sales figures."

"Bitch! That reminds me - are you onto Level 6 yet?" I asked, doing my lippy.

Our eyes met in the mirror and I knew that she was."

That evening I logged on. And for the method of destruction I chose 'Axe.'

"Level 6?"

I nodded. "I had to send out texts to other retribution members: Yes or No? All the texts came back with a Yes so I was through to the final stage. The instruction was to then log in immediately. It said I had 10 yes votes, and to click on the final stage - 'Confirm,' which I did. Goodbye, Tamsin. Now can I have a cup of tea, please? I've told you everything."

"Not yet. So what happened next? To Tamsin?"

"Where's Karen, by the way? Have you got her here too?"

"Safe."

"Where?"

"She's told us everything, Lily so there's no point in lying."

"Karen's sick in the head. You have to believe me. She's been sending the texts all along, hasn't she? And the emails. She made me do it. She's as mad as a snake. I'm glad I can see that now."

"Karen didn't receive any texts or emails, Lily. We've had her computer checked. She's clean."

There was a long pause while my world tipped on its axis. "What? So how did Tamsin? Oh God - so who...?"

"That's what we'd like to find out, Lily. Your computer is clean too. And your phone. So all this business about a site called Retribution is - how can I put this politely? Um - bullshit. So I'll ask you one more time, Lily - who tried to kill Tamsin Lewis?"

Swirling senses falling through space and time. None of this was real anymore. It didn't make sense what he was saying - no emails, no texts...And then it came to me - of course there weren't - all evidence would have been wiped. That was part of the deal.

"Who almost murdered Tamsin, Lily? You or Karen?"

"Almost?"

"And we're very angry about that."

I stared at him. He'd changed. Green eyes now and somewhat smaller.

"We've managed to wipe clean all yours and Karen's communication devices but the job still has to be completed. You and Karen slipped up somewhere and you're going to have to go through all 7 stages again. Only this time more carefully."

"Who the hell are you?"

"Once you've tapped into the laws of universal retribution the deed must be carried out or the consequences will be dire for all of us - do you understand? You are messing with Lucifer himself..."

This whole thing was worse than I could ever have imagined. Everyone around me was a lunatic. I hardly heard the rest of what he said over the thumping of my heart, filling my head, pounding through my veins.

"...Tamsin must die soon before she regains consciousness and talks. The axe missed her jugular..."

Wake up, Lily...wake up...

"You will now be taken for rest and then we will start again and next time you must succeed..."

Vaguely I remembered being removed by a couple of heavies, waking up in a room with faded orange curtains and someone sitting on my bed staring at me.

"You've been talking to yourself again," said the woman with red hair and a roll-up hanging off her lower lip. "All bloody night."

I sat up, looked around. The air smelled stale, like school dinners and pee. Oh yes. I reached over and checked. Phew. The blue tablets they'd given me for my so called psychosis were still safely stashed in my make-up bag. I'll be out of here soon and then I can finish the job. Because you can't mess around with the Universal Laws of Retribution. Tamsin Lewis *will* die. I promise you that.

Definition of schizophrenia: a mental disorder characterized by abnormalities in the perception or expression of reality. It most commonly manifests as auditory hallucinations, paranoid or bizarre delusions or disorganised speech and thinking in the context of significant social or occupational dysfunction. Onset of symptoms typically occurs in young adulthood with approx 0.4-0.6 of the population affected.

17
ROUGH LOVE

The front door slams. He leaves me crumpled on the stairs, staring bleak-eyed at the empty space he filled moments before: pointing, accusing, his beautiful mouth carved into a line of ugly contempt. But still there, imprinted on my world. And now he's gone.

Jay. A man impossible to second guess - from thunderous expression to disarming smile, soft caresses to an iron grip. His hungry stare lingers, haunting me, his steel embrace and panting breath hot on my neck...

Tears roll towards my ears, stinging, melting into my hair. So that's it. Over with one last slam. A slam so violent it makes the thin house tremble, a little more damp wallpaper slide down the walls and the bare light bulbs sway and flicker. How long I sit there I don't know. Cars whoosh past, spraying the pavements with diesel painted puddles, shadows play on the walls with the streetlights, and a long, long time later - the air around me darkens and chills.

The sheets are cold when I crawl in. They smell musty and faintly, ever so faintly, of Jay. Lying still and numb I stare with wide, sore eyes at the changing shapes on the ceiling - at blues and blacks and greys. A car door bangs, there's shouting in the street, a dustbin lid crashes. Some time around dawn, as ethereal fingers begin to poke through the slats of heavy cloud, a catfight pierces the silent gloom. Later, there are footsteps and a remote clicks open a car door. Gear changes fade into the distance. Perhaps I drift off - bizarre dreams tainted with an emotion I don't remember but which leaves me disturbed - but now there is more light. Doors open and close nearby. Newspapers snap through letterboxes. Another day. A day without him. Then another and another. The nights will be the worst.

***

"You need to see a doctor, Danielle," says my mother.

She's standing next to my bed with a cigarette hanging from her lower lip, arms folded. So she's back then from wherever she's been this time. She's got Kieren and Liam with her, I can hear them running rampage downstairs and tinkling animation coming from the TV. She reeks of nicotine and crisps and cheap perfume.

"It's no good turning away from me. Look at the state of you. You need help. It's not right, this isn't. Anyway, I've brought us some chips if you want some."

"I don't need a doctor." It's strange to speak, tongue and lips tripping over the words. "I just need time."

She turns to stare out of the window and takes a deep drag of her cigarette. The light is harsh, highlighting the crevices on either side of her mouth and around her eyes, her complexion sallow and lifeless. Her body is thin and rangy like mine, only kind of used-up looking and too stringy for the tight jeans and skimpy top she's wearing. The hair is yellow with black roots, like partially burnt corn, the heels of her cowboy boots worn down, nails bitten and hands as gnarled as ancient tree roots.

"Time," she says, as if seriously contemplating what I just said. She turns round. "I'm going down for my chips.

129

They'll be on the table in two minutes if you want some. Either that or starve. It's up to you, Danielle."

***

Some time after winter drags itself into the early days of spring, and bare branches forked against grey transform into shivering green arms, I open my bedroom window and lean out, breathing in the new air - earthy and slightly sweet mingled with petrol. I've spent my days and weeks spilling out of bed onto the sofa downstairs, trawling through shopping channels on the TV with glassy eyes, swilling bottled drinks then dragging myself back upstairs again. Music thumps through the walls and the boys fight like tigers. My mum's got a new boyfriend, Keith. I can hear the bed creaking again at night, muffled giggles and his mobile going off with its stupid frog tune. Always here with his big feet on the table, his bald pate shining in the light from the TV and his hairy hands on the remote. Outside, kids hang around in the street, cars rev, and life plays out around me, as if the shape that is me wouldn't matter if it was coloured in or not.

But this morning there is something different. Maybe it's the green shoots sprouting through the scruffy bit of lawn outside my window, the distant shouts from the schoolyard, or perhaps it's just time - the time I needed - but I want to go out. And now I've decided, I have to go. As I leave I catch sight of myself in the hall mirror - thin and ashen-faced, with a cheap pink anorak pulled over tracksuit bottoms and my hair scraped back in a ponytail. A walking stereotype.

The park is almost deserted. Litter flutters in tiny piles, flirting around bins loaded with cans and bags full of 'doggy-do' as little Liam calls them. Pit bulls mostly, round here. At this time of day the hooded teens are fast asleep and the only visitors are single mothers pushing buggies, their eyes hollow with exhaustion and hopelessness. I find a bench near the pond and sit down, ignoring the icy chill on my back, lifting my face to the weak rays of sunshine. If only Jude was here, my so called best friend who called round just once, said I was a 'Saddo' who needed to 'get a life.' It's like she's deleted me and there's nothing I can do about it.

A shout snaps me back and instantly I'm on alert. But it's only a woman chasing an errant puppy. The puppy is a chubby black and white spaniel with his tail held importantly high, eyes bright. He's chasing a leaf as it first rustles along the path then lifts into the air, twizzling round and round, dancing in the sunshine just out of his reach. The puppy pounces, misses, leaps and misses again. He spins around as finally the leaf floats away on a breeze, watching mesmerised and bemused, lost in his sweet and simple world. He had it and now he doesn't. Our eyes lock - his wide and brown and full of warmth and spirit - and something connects.

Then the woman reaches him, clips on a lead and the moment is gone. A moment that shifts the axis of my world so completely it is as if a switch has been flicked.

"Come on Harry, you naughty boy. I don't know. I let you off the lead for just one minute and….."

He glances back at me and I smile. Smile. For the first time in God knows how long. Because now I can see, really see. No one, I'm thinking, no one has the right to take purity and innocence, and turn it into despair.

***

The rage when it erupts is savage and vicious. "How dare you?" I shout, banging doors and pounding up the stairs.

She comes after me. "I'm in trouble because of you, Danielle. You're a bloody monster. I'm in court because of you."

She flicks ash on my bed and I swipe it off. I bare my teeth and spew my venom while she tries to slap me, over and over. Like she slapped me when I told her about Jay, when she didn't believe me, when she said I was a liar and a tart and a home-wrecker.

"Haven't you got to pick up Liam from nursery?"

She glares at me, forced to look at her watch. "I'll get Kerry to go from next door. You…" She points at me. "You need sorting."

It is two days later when I find out what this means. She's waiting for me when I get home from wandering round the park. We've had hail and sleet, my hands are mottled with purple and my lips are frozen. She is standing with her hands on her hips in the hallway, eyes narrowed to slits.

"Now you're fourteen, Danielle, it's been decided. You're going to your nan's to live."

I stare back at this woman who is my mother. Into the face that is sculpted, partly by character but mostly by experience, into aggression and defiance. She lifts her cigarette to her lips and inhales deeply, blowing a plume of smoke at the yellowing ceiling.

"You can get the bus this afternoon. I've packed your stuff. Maybe she can get you to go to school because I can't do a bloody thing with you and I'm in enough trouble as it is. I've given up, washed my hands of you, Danielle. I've got Kieran and Liam to think of now."

Not to mention Keith, I think, who's parked himself on our sofa to watch the racing while Liam sits eating a greasy packet of crisps for his lunch.

My nan has a one-bedroom maisonette with cardboard thin walls and the windows boarded up at the back because of repeated break-ins. A gang of yobs hang around outside on the triangle of mud that passes for a Green, burning tyres and swilling cider, threatening, jeering and intimidating those who fear them. Nan has a panic alarm and rarely leaves her home.

I stare into my mother's eyes and realise she doesn't give a damn. But it doesn't matter anymore: it's not her fault, not mine, not anyone's, just how it is. Wordlessly I shrug and clomp upstairs for the last time, pick up my holdall containing the few possessions I have and let myself out.

Needles of sleety rain sting my cheeks as I wait for the bus. I stamp my feet and I'm thinking - my life can go one of several ways now. I can get this bus or cross the road and get another. It rounds the corner, trundling towards me. Decision time. Seconds to go. Shall I get on it or not?

Nan will be waiting for me. Twitching the nets every few minutes. Probably she's made a cake and cooked a meal. My makeshift bed will be made up with clean sheets. And she doesn't' bring home tattooed men who swig from cans all day and creep into my bedroom at night. Telling me they love me. Messing with my head.
The bus screeches to a halt, the doors hiss open, and I get on it.

18
ROSIE AND JOE

Rosie stared through the stained glass of the magnificent oriel window in the Great Hall, and sighed at the darkening sky and flurry of dead leaves being chased across the lawns. A storm was blowing in, of that she was certain, and still no sign of visitors.

She looked over at the Grandfather clock tick-tocking methodically against the linen-fold panelling on the far wall - four o'clock - and walked over to prod at the log fire, which crackled and hissed in the grate. In the room across from the Hall, clattering crockery and raised voices signalled that preparations for tonight's dinner were already well underway.

Part of Rosie's job was to show visitors to Melhampton House their rooms upstairs. But time was pushing on and she'd been at work since early that morning. Rain had started to pelt the windows, splattering sideways in harsh bursts, leaving trails of rivulets to run down the panes. She threw another log onto the fire, thinking about the small room and single bed she would soon return to, and how lonely she sometimes felt in the long, dark winter nights, when a deep, male voice behind her left shoulder made her jump.

Rosie whirled round. 'Ooh, Sir, you gave me such a fright.'

The man laughed, throwing back a head of rich, black curls.

Rosie looked at him more closely, realising he was younger than she'd first thought - twenty, perhaps? Much the same age as herself, anyhow, and she felt a hot blush suffuse her skin.

'Joe,' he said, holding out his hand. 'Joe Rothwell.'

He gestured to one of the silk upholstered sofas either side of the fire, and they sat down, staring at the Flemish tapestry between them in tongue-tied silence.

Joe's physical presence seemed to fill the room, and Rosie felt her eyes being drawn to his. Immediately she looked away again, much to his obvious amusement. Oh dear, she should ask him something, like, 'where are the others?' or maybe introduce herself like she normally would, but every time she tried her throat constricted. The silence between them stretched and stretched, his warm, honey brown eyes searching her profile, willing her to look at him.

'You have a nasty cough,' he said.

'Have I?' She didn't realise she'd been coughing, since it was as regular as breathing these days.

The light outside was now fading fast, rain setting in, heavy and solid, dripping profusely from overflowing guttering and pipes. She ought to light the candelabra on the oak table. If only he wasn't staring quite so much. Eventually she forced herself to raise her eyes to his.

Joe smiled broadly. 'So, er…'

'Rosie.'

'How lovely. Rosie.'

Rosie blushed some more.

'Your name suits you. Ah hum… so they say this place is haunted. Is it true?'

'Oh yes,' said Rosie, slightly more comfortable now they were on her favourite subject - the history of the house. 'There's the Grey Lady. She's said to wander round the rose garden. And two gentlemen fighting a duel on the galleried landing. I've never seen them though, and I've been here for years.'

'Really? I've never seen you.'

'I've never seen you.' It felt as though she'd drunk a couple of glasses of strong wine too quickly, or woken abruptly from a dream - that feeling of static stillness, being aware of every thumping heartbeat, every firing nerve…..Who was this man who thought she should know him?

'I come here to visit Wills.' She barely registered what he was saying. 'He lets me use the Gatehouse to write in. I'm a poet. Perhaps I shouldn't say that, with only one collection published, or shortly to be…'

Joe. A poet…visiting…

A violent gust of wind suddenly whistled through the trees, thrashing the walls of the house and sweeping down the chimney so that smoke billowed into the room. Rosie began to cough again, and Joe jumped to her side and reached for her hand.   'Wild night.' He was oh so close, his hand folding her tiny cold one in his like a velvet glove. The desire to lean into him as if they had known each other all their lives was overwhelming. And really very, very silly.

Rosie stood up. 'Can I get you some tea, Joe?'

Joe blinked, long dark lashes feathering momentarily against ivory skin, the corners of his elegant lips twitching mischievously. 'Tea? How about some hot wine instead?'

Rosie pursed her lips. 'I'll bring tea.' Whatever would

the mistress say if she found her with a young man, drinking wine? Yet the smile she knew was spreading out across her face remained as she bustled through the 15th century archway to the ante-room, and from there down a spiral stone stairway to the kitchens.

Downstairs the intoxicating aroma of roasting venison and baked sponge filled her nostrils while she hunted for the tea set - people were always moving things to where she couldn't find them - and turned over in her mind the conversation with Joe.

Unnoticed amid the pandemonium in the kitchen, she made the tea, setting the tray with cream and sugar and a plate of scones and teacakes, then with trembling hands and racing heart, made her way back up to the Great Hall. Except for the fire, it was now quite dark. Quickly she set down the tray on the oak table in the centre of the room and lit the candelabra. 'There, that's better…'

But Joe had gone.

Rosie stared at the sofa where he'd been sitting only moments ago. Perhaps he'd sneaked off to the wine cellar next to the kitchen? Picking up the candelabra, she made towards it. The cellar, fully stocked and stacked with cases waiting to be unloaded, however, remained eerily quiet. Marching back into the Great Hall, she hurried up the spiral Jacobean staircase by the oriel window. The library was empty. As was the King's Room and the State Bedroom. She threw open every door down the corridor, flying from one room to the next - the Dressing Room, the secret passageway to the Chapel, the Yellow Room… knowing, yet needing to check anyway, that he wasn't going to be in any of them, that he had disappeared. Joe, quite simply, had disappeared.

And it was at that point, as Rosie resignedly plodded

back down to the Great Hall, that something he'd said began to replay in her mind: *Wills lets me use the Gatehouse*. She didn't know a 'Wills.' And secondly, and far more disturbingly - the Gatehouse was demolished in 1862, nearly forty years before.

***

Joe hurriedly let himself into the Gatehouse, bedraggled and soaked to the bones after his sprint outside. Rubbing his hands together he darted towards the small writing desk by the window, and quickly lit a candle so he could see to light the fire and search for that small bottle of brandy he knew he had somewhere. Finally slumping into the armchair by the fire he took a swig of liquor and forced himself to take calming, deep breaths. She was beautiful, the most exquisite creature he'd ever laid eyes on - flaxen hair, skin so translucent he couldn't stop staring at her - and yet...he'd known there was something odd about her, something ethereal, cold, unreachable. He took another long swig. Darn it, had she really walked straight through the wall? When his heart finally stopped banging against the wall of his chest, he shook his head. No, he'd been dreaming, tired after the long journey...what he'd do was go back and find out - he certainly couldn't let this rest.

***

Angela Phillips looked around at her assembled dinner guests in the Great Hall, and smiled. Everything was perfect - right down to the roaring fire and stormy night buffeting the 18 inch stone walls and rattling window panes. While the guests sipped mulled wine, she let her eyes roam around the 15th century Hall, noting the floor to ceiling family portraits of Nicholas's ancestors, who could be traced back for over five hundred years, the

Flemish tapestry over the fireplace and oh… a cold draught caused her to shudder. Strange, the heating was on full and the fire blazing.

'I hear you have ghosts?' A man was asking.

Laughter tinkled around the room as eyes turned towards her.

Angela smiled across at Nicholas and said, 'Of course we do. In fact We've got so many I'm surprised they don't bump into each other. There's the Grey Lady who wanders round the rose garden; a couple of gentlemen fighting on the landing; and a naughty housemaid who you can sometimes hear coughing - she leaves all the doors open upstairs as if she's looking for someone. And then there's a young man with heavy boots and wild black curls who stomps up and down the Great Hall here. Only on dark, rainy winter afternoons, though.'

'Like today.'

'Yes,' said Angela brightly. 'Exactly like today.'

19
COLD MELON TART

When I first saw Leo I did what everyone does - I flinched. It was like catching sight of someone reflected in the hall of mirrors. Poor guy, but then he must have become used to it over the years. All those double takes, frank stares and nudged ribs. *Look at him. Oh my God. Have you seen that*?

"Two espressos and a piece of your delicious melon tart, please," he said. Then, squinting at my name badge. "Thank you, Lucy."

"That's okay. Hot or cold?"

"Oh, cold."

I recovered myself quite well, I thought. Possibly because of the near murderous glare of the woman he was with. While he paid, he told her to find a table, that he'd bring everything over.

"Are you sure you don't want anything to eat?" he asked.

She pressed her lips together and gave a firm, little shake of her head before clattering off to a table in the far corner on ridiculous high heels. Ridiculous because her companion was so very short. Said a lot about her, those heels.

"So, you're new here?" he asked, over the hiss of the espresso machine.

I nodded, keeping the fixed grin on my face, trying not to stare. Just talk normally. "First day."

He paid and took the tray. "Don't worry, I'm sure You'll be fine. I can tell."

Martha, who was busy grinding coffee beans, shouted over her shoulder in mock horror. "Of course she will. I don't take on idiots, you know."

"I'm Leo, by the way," he said. "Everyone knows me. Once seen never forgotten, isn't that right, Martha?" His laugh rang hollow, tinkling in my head like ghostly children in an empty house.

From then on I saw him regularly. The thing was, I'd never come across anyone like him before. Ever. Oh, at school there'd been this boy who had to wear a wig and all the kids used to chant 'Wiggy' at him on the walk home. And in my class at University there's this girl with MS called Clare. But Clare's pretty and clever and doted on by everyone. The boys fall over themselves to carry her things and she has a specially adapted car and gorgeous clothes.

I looked down at the cheap black skirt I'd found in the sales, wiped my hands on the hugely unflattering red, checked apron I had to wear, and figured that we all had our burdens. Mine was paying for my education, hoping no one had stolen the food I'd bought from out of the fridge when I finally got back to the dingy terrace I shared, or nicked my drying underwear off the radiators. But nothing, nothing could be worse than Leo's burden. To have to live like that…

Usually Leo came in alone, sometimes with the woman I now knew as Tina. He always paid. No cover girl herself, she didn't treat him all that nicely, and it seemed to me that he was pitifully grateful to have her around at all. And she knew it. Covertly I'd sneak a glance at them while I cleared tables. He'd be chatting and she'd be staring at some place over his shoulder, not making any attempt to even pretend she was listening. I began to wonder if she was a resentful relative until I saw him reach for her hand one day, stroking the back of it over and over as if willing her to love him. To be honest, you know what I thought? I thought - what a bitch. For sure he didn't look good but presumably she knew that when she agreed to go out with him? For goodness sake, there was a human being under there. A really, really nice one too. A gentleman. Such a change from the sullen, hyper-critical boys I knew, who talked about girls like they were items chosen from a catalogue, swigged lager and never, ever asked you a single question. Perhaps being with him made her feel better about herself, and if so then she was even more of a...You know, I could feel my pulse bouncing along my arteries.

Maybe that's what started it. The fact that there he was, a guy not much older than me but with a warm, selfless personality despite his obvious afflictions - an innocent buffeted around by human inadequacies. Yet the barbs and taunts he must have suffered should surely have made him angry? I developed this sort of morbid fascination. Like, what *exactly* had caused his illness? And why didn't he do something about it?

I don't remember broaching the subject outright, but one day he was there on his own pushing a piece of melon tart around on his plate when we fell into conversation. Pleasant stuff, you know - just the weather and what I was studying. I liked that about him. That he was interested in what I had to say. Then it just came out - I don't think he meant it to happen but his misery was bubbling up long before it finally spilled over. He tried to contain it but it was clear he needed a friend.

"Tina's had enough."

Yes. I could have told him that weeks ago.

"They all do eventually. It's the NF." He pointed to the protrusion on his forehead.

"NF?" Well, I was studying English and drama not sciences.

He smiled indulgently. "Neurofibromatosis. It's where tumours grow in the nerve tissue. There isn't a lot you can do. I've had the worst ones removed but the one on my spine and here," he indicated a large cricket ball sized lump on the back of his skull and a smaller one protruding from his right jaw. "They're too dangerous to touch."

I nodded. Okay, so now I knew what to look up on the Internet. We chatted for several minutes about how amazed he'd been when Tina, who had sold him a small studio from where he worked as an architect, had got chatting to him and let him buy her lunch one day - he still remembered it, smiling while he stirred the refill of coffee I'd just poured. It had been a warm afternoon, and the café had been beside the canal, sunshine glinting off the water. A moment of precious time, captured forever in his memory. 'Normal,' was the word he used to describe how he felt that day. '*Almost* normal.' Then he snapped back to the present. "She's just met someone new, that's all. It happens."

I patted his hand. I had so many questions to ask but somehow the words jumbled in my mouth and wouldn't line up properly.

"Sorry," he said. "I do go on."

"No, no - not at all."

The man, I realised, was watching me carefully. "I think," he said, rubbing his jaw line. "That people just change."

You know I was bursting with compassion but it was all I could do not to dissolve, to keep the pity from my eyes. If I were him I would hate that. Imagine - either revulsion or pity from everyone who laid eyes on you? But it was difficult. And even more so when, on that last time he came in with Tina, I could see that his head was down while she, not even taking off her coat or touching her coffee, sat and stared at him. It occurred to me then to wonder how it might be for them in private. Had she been mean to him? I couldn't bear it.

Frankly I was relieved when, finally, their relationship was truly over and he began to come in on his own again, even though he looked pathetically downcast. He didn't want my sympathy, just a friendly word and his coffee and melon tart. But after that, a week or so, it began to get rather tricky.

I'll try to tell it exactly as it happened, but you must understand that the blinding flash of clarity I had all but eclipsed what happened first.

Well, here goes. I was tidying up after the lunch time rush one day, wiping down tables, clearing cups and plates, when I felt his eyes on me, following every move I made. And despite everything, the way he looked, I felt a tiny flutter of excitement. You have to realise he was an intelligent, sensitive, kind and funny man, with warm brown eyes that melted like chocolate. If it weren't for one tiny defect, a mutation of the NF1 gene, he would have been gorgeous. Well, anyway, I smiled back, one of those secretive this-is-just-between-us sort of smiles, a tacit communication that signalled complicity. And looking back there it was - that moment, that spark of pure egocentric stupidity - that one little thing we wish we hadn't done.

"Don't suppose there's any chance of a refill, is there?" he asked, indicating his empty cup.

I was due for class but I topped him up anyhow.

He smiled hopefully. "And another piece of melon tart?"

He must be feeling better, I thought, sliding the last piece onto a clean plate. That melon tart was the house speciality - short crust pastry, a custard base and dozens of honeydew melon balls crowded on top. It melted in the mouth and Leo loved it. Some people had it warmed up but it wasn't so nice that way. A bit gooey.

I brought it over and we got talking, just the two of us, while Martha washed up in the back kitchen. I remember the sun streaming in through the blinds, dust mites dancing in the slanted rays, the feeling that the afternoon was running past the window, leaving me behind on the warm, plastic coated bench, dozy, hypnotised, breathing in the heady aroma of espresso and re-heated croissants.

He took a sip of coffee through the side of his distorted mouth. Turned out he'd been to see his consultant that morning. "I've got another one coming," he explained. And for the first time I noticed a slight bulge at his left temple. "They're all growing and I've lost two more teeth on this side." Whenever he spoke the saliva flowed unchecked from the corner of his mouth causing him to dab at it constantly with a tissue. I knew by then, from researching his condition on the Internet, that things would worsen. And there was no cure.

A cold blast of air rushed across my back. Peering over my shoulder I noticed a young mother with a toddler in a pushchair. I'd turned quickly, in time to see the look of revulsion and horror that washed over her face when she caught sight of Leo. I said, "We're shut," coldly, unpleasantly, not like me at all. Our eyes locked and I could feel protective fury rising, glaring just like Tina had at me. After she'd gone, the whole incident only lasting a couple of seconds, I swivelled back round to see Leo spooning a piece of melon tart into the side of his mouth. He struggled to keep the mixture of saliva and custard from seeping back out, and a globule of custard oozed down his chin.

"I wondered," he said, putting down his spoon. "How you might feel about going to the theatre with me tomorrow night? I've got a spare ticket now that Tina…"
Martha had switched on the extractor fan and it's loud hum filled the room. Filled my head. You see, it was by then that I knew where this was going. And I also knew, in a flash of ice-sharp clarity, sitting there in the sun-warmed booth with the clanking of crockery and the whirring fan in the background, that to my utter shame, I couldn't do it.

20
LOOKING AFTER FRED

Wanted: House-sitter. Large, comfortable house. Own room and bathroom. Modest retainer fee to include light cleaning duties and looking after Fred.

***

When Peggy first encountered Fred on the stairs it wasn't pleasant. He nearly killed her. Frankly, it wasn't ideal to be living in an attic at her age, but if all she had to do to live in this lovely, rambling old house was a bit of dusting and feed the cat she couldn't really complain, could she? Nice little earner too. Yes, she'd really fallen on her feet here.

Still, there were some cats, Peggy thought, that you really couldn't take to - sly ones with sinewy bodies and howls like real babies; fiery tempered ones that sat in high places and swiped you with a fast left hook. And ones like Fred - hard cases with matted grey fur and pushed in faces - ones that slept all day then woke up around dusk for a night of brawling. However, Richard, the owner, seemed to love the brute enough to pay for a house-sitter to look after him, so she guessed it took all sorts.

Surely though… surely Fred couldn't be the only reason Richard wanted someone here while he was away? In Peggy's long career as a house-sitter she found there was invariably a reason people needed the house occupied.

It wasn't long before the kernel of curiosity inside her swelled and grew to such proportions that Peggy could stand it no longer. Richard had left the previous day, collected at some unearthly hour by a pinstriped gent in a smart car, and was not due back until the end of the week. She wouldn't be doing any harm anyway - just having a little look around - perk of the job - seeing who she was living with. She'd start with his bedroom.

Peggy's nose poked round the creaking door, her darting gaze taking in the neatly made-up double bed, drawn curtains, dust motes dancing in the sunlight through the gaps. Scooting past her swollen ankles, Fred pushed ahead of her and leapt onto the bed, immediately slinging a chunky thigh over his shoulder to wash his private parts. Peggy could see there were no cat hairs on that white bedspread. Now there would be. "Get off!" she hissed.

Fred stopped licking and a yellow stare met hers with an air of total disdain. Then he resumed licking.

Oh well. When she'd finished rooting around she'd boot him off with a cushion. Right now she'd really like to know what Richard did for a living. He'd told her he had overseas business, but of what nature? He could be leading a drug cartel or laundering money or dealing in stolen body parts for all she knew. This was for her own safety and peace of mind - after all, she was just a poor old lady up there in the attic all alone with no one knowing or even caring where she was.

Peggy's gnarled fingers rummaged through drawers and closets. The wardrobes revealed rows of Hugo Boss suits and jackets, silk ties and tailored shirts. Polished shoes were of hand-made leather and his underwear was Calvin Klein. He had several good watches and solid gold cufflinks, bank and building society books with healthy balances, and wads of cash rolled up in socks.

Peggy sat back on her heels and swallowed hard. His study was locked or she would have gone in there too. And so was the basement. This man was making money hand over fist, so much it was stashed everywhere. No wonder he needed someone guarding the house. Images of gun-toting rivals came riding into her wild imagination. Men in masks looking for money. She'd put a Yale lock on that attic door.

Meanwhile, what else was there she should know about? Pressing her nose up against the garage window she took in a gleaming Mercedes and a Harley. And in the lounge - the colossal plasma television. The only area he appeared not to have an interest in was the kitchen, which, Peggy thought, rather needed a woman's touch. She sat at the kitchen table sipping a cup of tea and dunking Richard's digestives, her great chest heaving with exhaustion after the morning's exertions. Having opened all the kitchen cupboards and seen the state of the fridge it was obvious her employer lived on beer and take-aways. Probably didn't have time, she thought, what with all the moneymaking schemes he appeared to have.

Her eyes widened as these thoughts processed - and that was something else, wasn't it? A middle-aged man with no wife, no partner and no girlfriend. Richard was definitely odd, and therefore before he returned it was vital to find out what he was up to. Her eyes flicked to the locked cellar door. And whatever it was - she had a feeling she would find it down there.

Peggy poured herself another cup of tea. That lock

was a sophisticated one and this might take some time. But there had yet to be one she couldn't unpick. She glanced at the clock on the wall - less than 48 hours before her employer came home. Best get it over with, especially if she had to make a quick get-away. No joke at her time of life. Not to think about all that now, of course. There was a job to be done.

Fred sat on the kitchen table with his tail thumping while she worked. It had been surprisingly easy and once the bolts were released the cellar door sprang open. Peggy peered down into the darkness, taking tentative steps and fumbling with her arthritic fingers for a light switch. Aha - she'd found it. The basement flooded with light. And that's when she had her second encounter with Fred on the stairs. At the precise moment Peggy put out her hand to grab the stair rail, Fred bustled past, bumping the backs of her legs on the narrow step and knocking her off balance.

The last thing she remembered before pain seared through her ankle and the crack on her head knocked her out, was Fred springing up to a small barred window and squeezing himself out into the sunlight.

***

When Richard arrived home the following evening he wasn't best pleased. First he'd had to take that darned old biddy to the hospital and now he had to hire a locksmith and find a new house-sitter. All because that silly, old woman couldn't keep her nose out of someone else's business. Still, at least she was alive. A few days in for concussion and a broken ankle and she'd be returned from whence she came, thank goodness. Especially since he'd found out all the woman's references were fake and her real name was Hetty Buttersworth. An ex-petty thief no less, and of no fixed abode. Next time he'd have to be more careful and phone the previous employers.

Darned nosy house-sitters. A necessary evil. But Fred was pretty special - his late wife, Anne, had adored that cat - pleading with him to take care of Fred when she'd gone. And he couldn't risk a burglary. Particularly in the basement. That evening a new advertisement went into the local gazette.

***

Wanted: House-sitter. Large, comfortable house. Own room and bathroom. Modest retainer fee in exchange for light cleaning duties and looking after Fred. References will be checked.

***

The whole episode had set him back by almost a week. Without Anne, he was able to accept all the new business deals that came his way, and jobs were pouring in. Before that all the money had come from Anne. The sole heir from a wealthy family she held all the purse strings and she hadn't liked him leaving her alone - one of the reasons he'd bought her Fred to keep her company so he could leave the house once in a while. Still, she was gone now. But Fred wasn't and with three weeks in the States coming up, it had been crucial to sort out the house-sitter problem. And now, finally, it looked as though he had.

Amy was a small, skinny girl who was studying design at the local college and desperately needed a place to live where she could work in peace. She'd been delighted with the attic room all to herself and made a big fuss of Fred. Richard smiled as he snapped shut his briefcase and let himself out into the crisp, grey dawn. Eight hours from now and he'd be in New York, safe in the knowledge that all was finally well again at home.

But for Amy, all those locks on the doors were simply too much. At first she was thrilled not to be sharing crummy digs, to have enough money to eat properly and a lovely bed to sleep in. But after a week in the cavernous, silent house, it was almost as if those closed, locked doors were whispering every time she passed - *look inside, look inside...* What if this man was a mass murderer and behind those doors were walls plastered with photographs of murdered girls, unsolved crimes, trophies on display? Here she was alone, a slip of a girl with family far away. She really ought to know. It would be stupid not to.

The locks were big ones. And way too complex. Besides, if she broke one of them she couldn't afford to replace it, and if the owner found out he might evict her or worse... She pictured being throttled in the kitchen. Richard was a bear of a man and his eyes were too close together. No. Forget it.

But as the hours ticked by the whispers grew louder, interrupting her thoughts whenever she tried to study or relax. That evening she lay on the sofa reading and re-reading the same paragraph while Fred sat on the floor eyeing her jangling bracelets.

Finally she put her book down. "What do you think, Fred? Is your master a mass murderer?" She reached out to stroke him.

Fred's pupils dilated and suddenly he leapt for the bangles with both paws, fastening his claws around her arm. He would have told her if he could. But right now he was busy drawing blood.

Amy got busy, trying to put all suspicious thoughts out of her mind. She studied. Dusted. Vacuumed and tidied. One thing that was truly lovely about this old house was the garden and tomorrow she'd prune the roses. Actually no, she'd do it now while the late afternoon sun was still out. It would take her mind off the nagging voice in her head that said she was living with Jack the Ripper - *A fortnight until he's due home...you could break those locks...*

Amy swept the patio. It was a while since anyone had given this garden any attention. Such a shame. The man was obviously a workaholic. This place needed a woman's touch. Odd that - no wife, no partner and no girlfriend. A shiver ran up and down her back while she reflected on that. About the same time as something glinted in the sun. Fred's nametag. And that was the first time she noticed the cellar window.

Amy crept towards it, broom in hand. It was half-moon shaped with three bars across, but as she bent to look inside, Fred swiftly shot past her and smoothly slipped in through a gap underneath. Amy gasped. A tomb like chill emanated from the cellar and she couldn't see in, but what she could do was squeeze through the same hole. In the grip of excitement, she dropped the broom and flattened her body to the floor, then wriggled and poked her head through. This, if she could just get in, would be the ideal solution. No lock breaking and she could put her mind at rest.

But as she heaved and pushed her way in, it soon became obvious that the gap was much too narrow and she was pretty much stuck. What a mess she was in. The neighbours were acres away in a salubrious suburb like this and besides, night was closing in. A surge of panic swelled up inside her. One last attempt and then she'd have to start screaming for help. One last push.

Then suddenly she was in. The drop was considerable and she fell in a crumpled heap onto cold flagstones with pain screaming through her left arm. Slowly, Amy tried to adjust to the solid wall of blackness. That darned cat had led her in here. What a crazy thought to have at a time like this. But even so - she could swear he'd deliberately brought her here. So why?

Gripping her elbow, she considered the options. No one would hear her scream. Richard would not be back for weeks. She had no phone and the door was locked, even if she could manage to find and climb the attic steps. She put her head in her hands and bit back the sobs. All she'd wanted was a bit of peace and quiet and the chance to study. But because she'd suspected a perfectly decent man of being a murdering savage she was in this terrible mess.

Finding a cloak of something she thought might be tarpaulin to wrap herself in, for now all she could do was survive the night. In the morning there would be some light and she could think again.

Dawn came early with slats of ghostly grey through the barred window. And a pair of yellow eyes staring in at her. Fred. Of course! Amy sat up. If she got him to come to her she could tie something to him like a note and then someone would find her.

"Here puss! Here puss, puss. Oy Fred!"

Fred stared at her and then began to methodically wash his chest.

"Fred! Come on! Come to me. Here puss, puss, puss."

Fred stopped licking. Considered the proposition. Then resumed licking.

Another hour passed with the day brightening steadily, illuminating the cellar. Amy looked around for something she could stand on, straining to hear what she thought were a couple of voices coming from next door, an open window maybe? And that was when she noticed the recently disturbed stones. So there *was* something here!

Crawling forwards, she could see now that the dirt around the cracks was relatively fresh. Once again the thought occurred - *Fred had brought her here.* This was a secret. And she had to know what it was.

She clawed away the dirt and eased up the first stone. The first thing she saw was long dark hair. The next swirling, head-spinning blackness as she flew back against the wall and screamed for help. It was a woman. The wife?

She looked up. Met with a pair of yellow eyes. And then with a flick of a tale Fred disappeared into the sunlight. Someone, at last, had found his mistress. Job done.

21
NIGHT DUTY

Strange things happen in hospitals during the early hours. I should know - I've been working nights for long enough.

There's something timeless about the long, grey hours of dawn that makes people feel disorientated: who are they? Where are they? Often I'd be on my rounds and find a befuddled patient in the sluice looking for a kettle! Or determined to get dressed because they're late for work. It would take a minute before they remembered - oh yes, still in hospital, got a drip up. Back to bed. Back to sleep. Just a bad dream.

Tonight Tessa's in charge. She sits knitting - click-clack-click-clack - and chatting to the tea-lady, Beryl, who's just finished washing up the cocoa mugs. Leaving me, as usual, to walk round and check up on the patients. Tessa, to be blunt, is lazy - she works a couple of nights a week for the better rate of pay, then does as little as possible while she's here. She's not dedicated like me. For me this is a vocation: a calling. The way it should be.

First there's old Mr Betts - in my opinion they should never have operated at his age. At home he could manage but now he's got a nasty chest infection and doesn't know where he is. They asked him, shouting into his one good ear, "Do you know where you are, Arthur?"

"Aye," he shouted back. "I'm in bed."

Not lost his fighting spirit then!

On a waiting list, he's now down for residential care. Gaunt and wheezy, he lies staring at the ceiling, listening to the hiss of oxygen and asking for his late wife.

"Where's my Lily? Are you Lily?"

I squeeze his hand. "Lily's here."

It's best.

And then there is Isobel. Isobel was a lively schoolteacher. Now look - with creeping inevitability, Isobel is fading to grey, her cold, tissue fingers reaching for mine. I'm glad I'm here, whispering, reassuring, to take her through the darkest hours.

I end with Joe in the side ward - there because he relives the battlefields, groaning and shouting. It keeps the others awake.

"Joe. I'm here now. It's all right."

His young, hazel eyes widen, confused and then relieved. It's just night time. "Don't leave me, Nancy. Stay with me."

I pull up a chair and hold his hand. "Of course."

"Promise?"

Tucking in his blankets, I whisper, "Promise." When I finally drift back to the nurse's station, Tessa is telling the night sister ghost stories. The poor night sister will later have to walk alone down the draughty corridors of the old District General as she visit's the other wards, her footsteps echoing eerily on the cracked tiles. At each sigh of wind or rattling window pane, she will shoot nervous little glances over her shoulder - walking quickly past the operating suites, now acutely aware of the patient who once escaped from the morgue, and the vengeful hospital porter who stalks the deserted basement. She shudders as

Tessa laughs gleefully - clickety-clack-clickety-clack.

"How's Arthur Betts?" Sister asks, checking her notebook.

Tessa carries on knitting. "Oxygen on. Propped up. Obs okay."

Sister nods. "Isobel?"

"Yeah, fine."

"And how's the heating in those side wards? Is it fixed yet? Have we got enough blankets?"

Behind Sister I shake my head but Tessa ignores me. "Still freezing. We've got blankets, though. We've done our best."

I glare at Tessa as she peers over Sister's shoulder and frowns at me.

"Well, best get on," says Sister. "Wish you hadn't spooked me, though. I'll be terrified all night now."

Tessa laughs and carries on knitting. Eventually she looks at her watch and stretches. "Oooh - time for a break," she says, wandering into the kitchen to make herself a coffee.

A break!

In the day room sit the insomniacs, watching shadows flicker along the walls. Outside, fog swirls around buttery lamplights and dark streets glisten damply. Huddled in dressing gowns the talk is of loosely grasped politics and lives of rough work, jobs which have left them with hardened lungs, greying skin and hollow eyes. I pull my cloak around me and settle into one of the armchairs at the back of the room for forty winks. Five o'clock: always the most difficult time to stay awake. The two old men, muttering about the cold, shuffle back to their plastic mattresses and thin sheets. Strange, this hour between night and dawn: with the body slow and the mind playing tricks.

I drift in and out of a dream-filled slumber, suddenly jumping alert with a feeling of déjà vu. Still dark out there, but silvery fingers are creeping through the blinds and there comes the distant rattle of the medicine trolley. It must be six o'clock. Goodness - Tessa is doing some work! Tea-cups rattle and beds creak as sleep-fuddled patients struggle to prop themselves up or plod towards the bathroom. Lights flick on. Blinds roll up. A new day.

Sometimes I feel so darned weary I could just roll over and forget the world, but there is work to be done. And my first thought is Joe.

He's fast asleep. For once no murmurings or kicking. I tuck the blankets back up to his chin and sit watching him for a while. Okay, you've gathered - I've got a soft spot for him. But Joe is the reason I became a nurse - to look after people damaged and traumatised. Who else is going to care for him like I do? Who else will sit through the night and hold his hand when he cries out? Most nurses would rather be at home with their families or tucked up in bed asleep. There aren't many like me these days.

Tessa, having dispensed the medicines and filled in a few charts with fictional temperatures and blood pressures, pens the notes (slept well, slept well, slept well...) before disappearing for a quick breakfast prior to the day staff arriving.

Me? I move on to Isobel and old Mr Betts. They are tired now. The night has been a long one. Tea cups sit untouched and I pull up blankets, smooth brows and let them sleep on. My work is done.

At the end of the shift, I'm in Sister's office when the door opens.

"She was here again last night," says the night sister to the day sister. "I'm sure of it."

"Who? The Angel?"

Night Sister nods. "The two old chaps in the dayroom said the air was freezing in there."

"The heating has gone again, Sister."

"I know - but both Mr Betts and Isobel dying in one night? And some of the patients said they saw a figure drifting around the beds in a long dress. And that side ward is perishing. No wonder no one will sleep in there. Poor Beryl dropped the tea-tray again this morning - said she saw a grey figure slip out through the door!"

"I think Tessa's been up to her old tricks again with those ghost stories - you look as white as a sheet. Both of those patients were extremely ill! Have the relatives been told? Good. Anyway, you know how it is in the early hours with strange noises and apparitions! Strong painkillers or a few stories and everyone thinks they can see ghosts on the ward."

Well she's right there, I think. They certainly do. And I should know. I've been here for over seventy years now. I've seen enough startled faces and mouths dropping open to know for sure that they do.

I'm going to leave them now to discuss their ghosts. For me it's back to the side ward to sit with Joe. He needs me and I'll always be here for him. Waiting. Willing him to recover. I promised.

He begged me all those years ago. In his darkest hour. "Don't leave me will you, Nancy? Promise You'll be there when I wake up?"

"Of course I will." He was the reason I came here, like I said. We were going to marry before the second world war broke out, you see.

And I never break my promises. I'll never leave my Joe.

22

SIXTY SECONDS

60 seconds and the whole thing will be over. Helen bites her lip and grips the steering wheel. *Do it. Time's running out. Just do it...*

Kirsty steps off the pavement, blonde hair curling in the early evening drizzle. She turns to face the oncoming traffic. *Do it - Now!*

***

They'd been at school together and only re-met when Kirsty brought her elderly aunt in to the nursing home that Helen managed.

"Come and have a drink after work," said Kirsty, wandering round Helen's office, picking up ornaments then putting them down again - not quite in the same place they'd been before. Her gaze eventually settled on a photograph of Helen's son. "Now there's a handsome boy."

Helen smiled proudly. "My son, Jamie. He's off to university next month."

"Yours and Rob's boy? Well, well - Rob always did have good looks. You dropped lucky there, Helen."

Helen's smile faded a little.

"Anyway, must dash. Things to do and all that. Come if you can - it would be lovely to have a catch up!"

Kirsty's stilettos click-clacked sharply across the foyer.

An engine roared to life outside the window. Gravel flew. And the day darkened.

The afternoon was a busy one with several new admissions followed by a fire in the kitchen. And at six o'clock, Helen's reflection in the office mirror told her that an early night would be a far more sensible option than going to a city bar to meet an old school friend she hadn't seen in over thirty years. Especially such a glamorous one - wouldn't she feel a frump?

Rain spattered against the windows, and the aroma of boiled vegetables and gravy wafted down the corridors in a pungent reminder of school days. She and Kirsty had never even been close. Kirsty was the girl who whispered behind your back making another girl giggle. Then she'd grin and say, "What? I didn't say anything!"

Kirsty had been the first girl in class to get white, knee boots. The first to own a record player. And the first to be kissed by Darren Mathews, a tough boy with dark hair and a dimpled grin. All the girls wanted to be kissed by Darren but Kirsty was the one he chose. Or did he? With the benefit of hindsight, Helen wondered about that.

Still - it would be nice to find out what had happened to some of her old classmates, and she could hardly leave the poor woman waiting alone in a city centre bar, could she? Helen fluffed up her short, greying hair as best she could and applied a smudge of lipstick. She'd go.

But it wasn't until the occasional catch-up had turned into regular drop-ins that she became suspicious. They had little in common - Kirsty was a childless divorcee with a high-powered career - and few shared interests, Kirsty being into fashion and parties, and Helen preferring to garden or read.

Then one day when Helen was bending over the

weekly staff rota deep in thought, Kirsty bounced into her office for the fourth time that month. Helen took off her glasses and suppressed a deep sigh.

"Just popped in to see Auntie," said Kirsty. "Thought I'd say hi. So, how are you, Helen?" She flung herself onto the chair opposite and plonked her designer handbag on the floor. "You look dreadfully tired, dear. You ought to treat yourself to a facial. I swear by them."

"Kirsty!" said Helen through gritted teeth. "How nice to see you."

"Shall we get some coffee? Will someone bring us some?"

"I'll get it. Sugar?"

"God, no!"

"So how are things, Kirsty?" Helen looked at her watch. She really was extremely busy. "I've got a few minutes for a break but not long if you don't mind."

"Not at all." Kirsty took off her long, cream coat and tossed it onto the sofa behind her. "Truth be told I just need someone to talk to. Other women are always so busy with their boring family squabbles…" Here she raised her eyes to the ceiling. "…and I've split up with Carl. Do you remember me telling you about him?"

Helen took a sip of coffee and tried to recall who Kirsty's latest boyfriend was. Something about him being a student or having a lot in common with her son, Jamie, and wouldn't it be great if they could meet up? Something like that. She did know she'd managed to avoid the foursome where her son would be the same age as Kirsty's partner. At least now that particular nightmare - where she and Rob would feel like elderly relations - was over.

She tuned back in while trying to keep an eye on the

clock. All the medicines still had to be dispensed to the residents and she had an appointment with a catering manager in less than an hour.

"...so I was wondering if I could stay over at yours for a while. At least until he's gone. I've told the boy to be packed and out within the week. All the tears and tantrums, honestly, when a relationship's run it's course, it's run its course..."

Helen frowned. This boy was only a couple of years older than Jamie. Perhaps Kirsty had forgotten how raw feelings could be at that age. Jamie had split with his girlfriend last summer. She recalled his wracking sobs through the bedroom walls. When she went into his room he'd reached out to her like a broken child and she'd rocked him to sleep. After that he refused to go to university, get a job or even go out with his friend, Steve. It had taken months for him to agree that his life mattered and the decisions he made now would have a lasting impact.

They were now on solid ground again but his emotions still swung alarmingly. Poor Carl. She hoped he had somewhere to go.

"...and what I can't stand about him is the way he just stares at me. I said, 'It's like, so over. Get a life. Time to move on.' What a body though! Helen - don't look so shocked." Kirsty glanced at her watch. "Oops, look at the time." She reached for her coat. "So if I come over on Friday? About six? I'll take you and Rob out for dinner, of course."

Annoyance clouded Helen's features as more smiles and air kisses were bestowed on her. At what point had she agreed to this? Talk about being shunted into something. Still, just a few days, she'd said. What harm could it do? As long as Kirsty didn't get her painted talons into Rob: her good-looking, charming, far too easy-going husband.

Rob. She'd been looking in the wrong direction. By the time Helen knew for sure that Kirsty was seeing Jamie, it was too late. During her time with them Kirsty had behaved impeccably. Arriving with a huge bouquet of flowers for Helen and two bottles of red wine for Rob, she had pretty much kept to her room after taking them out for dinner. On Sunday she'd disappeared to her parents' for lunch and by Tuesday she had gone, leaving a box of chocolates and an envelope with a fifty-pound note tucked inside.

At the time they'd been pleased.

But Kirsty's work had been done. Executed with all the swiftness of a trained assassin. A flash of kohl rimmed eyes over the dinner table. A red stiletto. An open dressing gown. Jamie. She had his number.

She'd been watching Rob. Watching to see if his eyes brightened when Kirsty walked in the room, how attentive he was, if his mood altered when Kirsty left. It wasn't Rob.

Initially it was Kirsty's absence from the nursing home - Aunt Martha had been abruptly and ruthlessly abandoned. Then Jamie's coy reaction to her question about who he was seeing one evening. Followed by a casual slip of a remark about older women. A sly smile. A furtive mobile phone conversation. Kirsty. She knew it.

It was around that time that Helen started having evil thoughts. They came when least expected - shooting across her brain like poisonous darts. Sometimes they happened just as she was falling asleep, other times she'd be leaning over someone's bed, tucking them in. In a flash would come an image: Kirsty held at gunpoint; Kirsty drowning - face bloated and gasping; or lying broken and bent like a puppet after tripping down a flight of steps; or maybe stuck in a lift that was plummeting to the basement….

And once they started they wouldn't stop. She'd be spooning out fruit salad when whoosh – Kirsty's parachute cord failed. Administering insulin when bam – Kirsty's plane hurtled into the side of a mountain. Sipping tea with bereaved relatives when alas, poor Kirsty choked into her poisonous mushrooms. Like a door that had opened slightly her visions kept coming, slipping through the gap until she could no longer control them, couldn't sleep nights, her head hurt and her eyes burned.

***

So here she is after waiting round the corner from the wine bar in the tomb like stillness of her parked car. Fingers and toes numb, teeth chattering, she has watched Kirsty and Jamie leave the bar together, his arm around her shoulder while she chats on the phone to someone else, shrugging Jamie away.

Last night Jamie told her he was leaving home - moving in with someone and not going to university. He didn't want to do what she wanted him to do - needed to do his own thing. He'd slammed his bedroom door. Started packing. Wouldn't say where or who or why…It couldn't happen, that's all she knew. Kirsty was not going to use her son, spit him out and ruin his life. The engine screams. *Do it…now!*

The sharp rap at her window causes her heart to jackhammer against her ribs and the car slams to a halt. "What the hell do you think you're doing, Woman?"

A man is shouting through the steamed up passenger window. "You nearly killed me."

Helen squints up at him. He is on a bike, gesticulating madly. She glances ahead. In time to catch Kirsty wrenching open the door to her car and jumping in. Headlights flood the wet tarmac as she vanishes into the traffic.

Helen buzzes down the window. "I'm so sorry. I didn't see you."

The man glares and then relents. "All in one piece. Just remember to use your mirrors next time, okay?"

Helen nods. A horn peeps. Fresh air fills the car. That man on the bike has saved them all. Rob. In her mind she sees Rob's face, ashen and drawn, as she is led away to a police car. Hands shaking violently, she grips the steering wheel and starts the engine. Deep breaths. How close she came. It was planned. Would have been murder. Deep breaths. Cold rain on her skin. And then a movement in the shadows catches her eye.

She recognises his huddled shape in the bus shelter. Swinging the car round to a blasting of angry horns, Helen pulls alongside him. They drive for a few minutes in silence before Jamie says, "Not really her night, was it?"

"Pardon?"

"First me dumping her and then you trying to run her over."

Confusion clouds her thoughts. "But, I thought…"

"I didn't dare tell you. Me and Steve want to backpack for a year. She didn't like it either."

"And it's Steve you're moving in with, not…"

A cold sweat breaks out down Helen's back, washing over her in a shudder. If she ever saw that man on the bike again she'd have to pin him to the ground and kiss him.

23

THE EXTRACTOR

England February 2012

Eve lay back in the dentist's chair and concentrated on her breathing. There was nothing to be afraid about. The days of gas masks, blood and pliers had long been consigned to history. This was a 21st century private dental practice 'specialising in the care of nervous patients.' She'd be fine.

The dentist, Max, who possessed a brilliant set of fridge-white veneers and an air of nonchalance, smiled down at her, blue eyes twinkling. "Now what flavour local anaesthetic would you like, Eve? Amaretto, spearmint, raspberry, strawberry...lemon, gin and tonic..."

"I'll have spearmint, thanks."

"Excellent choice. Now open wide, poppet. That's a good girl." He called to his assistant, a sultry girl with a mass of dark hair and brilliant green eyes - so green Eve decided they were contacts. "Get the vibrator, would you, April?"

Eve giggled.

"What we do is hook this little device over your lip and it will vibrate against your gum, so your brain is tricked into ignoring any pain. Just another brilliant invention to make this all completely painless for you."

Eve began to relax. She'd got to have this back molar out and the dread that had been building over the past few weeks finally began to ebb away. The pain was going to be eradicated forever. No more excruciating toothache when she bit down. It would soon be over.

Out came the needle. Quite a big one, she noticed. *Calm down...deep breaths...*She wouldn't feel a thing...

"Just relax, Gorgeous," came the soothing sound of Max Coldman's voice. "There's a poppet..."

The pain ripped through her jaw. Unexpected. Howling. *Fucking hell...*

She tried to say it was hurting, gesticulating madly, but her mouth was wedged open and no sound came. The huge needle plunged into her gum, sinking deeper and deeper, until it must surely have reached her neck. Quickly withdrawn, another, much larger syringe - so large he could barely hold it in one hand - was flourished, and this time injected into the inside of her gum, pointing to the back of her mouth and downwards into the main nerve.

No, no...stop...stop...

A cramp-like pain shot across to the jaw and up the side of her face into the temples. She broke a sweat. Started to shake. Heart pumping so fast she thought it would trip into fibrillation.

"Want a window open, Sweetheart?"

He was a nice man. Obviously he hadn't waited long enough for the local to work before he put the needle in. It would kick in soon. Anytime now. She had to be brave. *Mustn't be a baby. Breathe. Just breathe...*

April, the assistant's, green eyes flickered in and out of focus as she hovered with the suction tube.

Eve tried again to speak, to motion to the assistant, to

say it hurt like hell, but Max was back. He drew his chair closer. "Now, think of this as a row of roses and the middle one's being dug up with a spade. You'd rock it a bit first, wouldn't you? Loosen things up? Well that's what we're going to do now. Let me know if you feel anything."

He had a pair of massive pliers. Shitting hell. Wedged into her mouth.

Eve's stare was eyeball wide as she watched, felt the rocking and tugging. It would be all right. Soon the anaesthetic would kick in. And what about the nerve block? You weren't supposed to feel anything, surely? She gripped the chair. Breathing deeply. Watching.

There was the sound of a crack - like snapping bone. And then another.

Max held up a piece of enamel and passed it to April.

"More suction?" said April.

He nodded. "Keep it there. Aha - another piece. Hmm. Tricky customer, you are Eve - I'm afraid we're going to have to drill the rest of it out. But We'll do it in two parts. Just let me see if we can have another little go...aha...lovely jubbly..."

April's green eyes darkened.

Eve gripped the chair until her nails screamed. Sweat poured down her back. On and on and on went the deep, throbbing, rocking sensation as Max worked with the pliers. She watched the hands of the clock tick slowly round the dial - twenty minutes had passed - and still her jaw held on to the tooth. Blood trickled down the back of her throat. Suction popped at her tongue. On and on and on with the pliers.

Finally Max sighed and shook his head, "Okay - We'll have to do a tiny bit of drilling, my lovely. Nothing to worry about. Sometimes they're harder to get out than others, that's all. Open wide again, there's a poppet."

The drill whirred into life. Then screeched into the socket. Bone was blasted, nerve endings annihilated, blood vessels shattered. She tried to lift up her hands but they weighed like lead.

Briefly she lost consciousness. When she opened her eyes again another six minutes had ticked by. Still he was drilling. Water and spit and blood flew over her face. Max had one knee on her chair, his full body weight bearing down on her jaw, forcing the drill ever deeper into bone. On and on. She blacked out several more times. Tears dripped into her hair.

Then, just like that, it stopped. It was out. She'd been an hour in the chair and on the little table next to her was a pile of tiny dental chippings. About twenty. Not two parts. Twenty…

Eve sat shaking, shivering. Tried to get out of the chair but couldn't.

"Hmm. Still a bit of root left in there, my darling," said Max. "Only a few more minutes and We'll have the little devil out."

The next size up in the drill category came out. It looked like something you'd use on a wardrobe. Eve dug into the chair with her nails. Concentrated on breathing. It couldn't last forever. Soon she'd go home and take a mountain of painkillers and that would be that.

Once more blood clogged her throat. Pain pulsed down her neck. Screwed into her head. Thudded heavily in her gums. Her eyes rolled in their sockets like a frightened mare. Her lips and jaw muscles unable to move.

Unable to move…Oh My God!

The realisation suddenly hit her - she hadn't uttered a word of protestation because ...*she couldn't*!

"Bet you wish you were somewhere else right now, don't you?" Max chuckled.

He'd got that right.

But her slight nod seemed to trigger something. April seemed mesmerised. Her green eyes unnervingly brilliant - glittering like emeralds in the sun. And Max - his jolly blue eyes glinting with rubies...as he climbed further onto her chair and pinned her with his entire weight, prising open her jaw wider and wider so the drill disappeared inside her mouth ...*high-pitched screeching mingled with...oh my God...laughter...April was laughing!*

The next thing she recalled was being led into the reception room, her legs trembling violently, and being advised to 'take it easy for a day or two'.

"You might need to pop a Nurofen before bedtime," said Max. "Otherwise, start using your mouthwash tomorrow. Oh, and you might want a little towel on your pillow in case hubby thinks you've been at the red wine again!"

Wiping his hands, he nodded to the receptionist. "If she faints just stick her head between her legs."

The receptionist looked up. "That'll be £120 please, Eve Sweetheart."

***

Over the next few days the pain got steadily worse. Eve knocked back wall-to-wall diclofenac, codeine, paracetamol and some of her best friend's Tramadol. She used mouthwashes every hour and couldn't eat. Her jaw swelled to twice its size. As each analgesic wore off she counted the minutes until she could take something else. Pulsing, deep throbs radiated down her jaw and into her neck. She'd never liked whisky but now she swigged it back, ignoring the stomach pains, immune to the rising nausea.

Her neck began to spasm. The socket, stitched, became infected. Nerves jumped - waking her in the early hours with electric shocks, which contracted for minutes at a time until all she could do was ball up in a corner of her bed and whimper. Too shocked and scared to cry. Hell, she couldn't relax enough to cry, or the electric shocks would start again. All night vigilance and a timetable of drugs became the norm.

"Well you have to go back and get some antibiotics. Get him to put it right." Everyone said it.

Go back there? Are you fucking kidding me?

At 3.45 am one morning three weeks later, Eve was air-lifted to hospital in a coma while her husband frantically explained what had happened.

A severe jaw infection was diagnosed and IV antibiotics initiated immediately. A kindly maxillo-facial surgeon explained as they rushed her to theatre that nothing more would be done to her while she was awake. That was the last she remembered.

***

It was six months before Eve could even talk about it. A week in hospital had saved her, but even months later she still woke in the night convinced the electric shocks would start again in her mouth. She'd had to have all three molars removed and part of her jaw bone. And she still took analgesics. And time off work. And anti-depressants.

"You should sue the arse off him," said her best friend, the one who had supplied her with extra strength codeine and Tramadol during her darkest hours.

Eve nodded. She'd never sued anyone before. He'd done his best to get it out, hadn't he? Surely it was her own fault for not taking antibiotics - for not going back?

"Sue him," said her step-mother.

"Sue him," said her auntie.

"Sue him," said her husband.

And so she did. A few days later, Eve picked up the phone to one of the many law firms offering the service. Shocked, and sure of compensation, they stepped on the case straight away. And a week later they rang back. Unfortunately there wasn't a dentist called, 'Max V. Coldman.' Anywhere.

Eve held the telephone to her ear. A cold chill swept through her veins like tumbleweed down an empty corridor. "But I went there," she explained. "I gave you the address, the phone number. He had an assistant called April Vine. I can describe him. Unfortunately."

"I'm sorry," came the genuinely regretful voice. "There is no practice registered at that address and no dentist of that name anywhere. We've got all your hospital records but nothing before that."

Eve shot from the house and jumped into her car. Screeched out of the drive. They were so wrong. But on arrival at the dental surgery, the windows were boarded up, weeds grew in between the paving on the driveway, and the sign creaking on the chain was covered in graffiti. He'd gone.

"But why?" her best friend asked. " Incompetence? A deluge of court cases? Well at least he won't be able to do it to anyone else. At least he's dismissed and taken off the register or whatever - that'll be why they can't find him on it."

Eve nodded. "Yeah. But they should still be able to

trace him and they say they can't. They even put the police onto it - but he's vanished. Gone. Totally."

***

<u>Los Angeles: March 2013</u>

In the private Ophthalmology waiting room, Scarlett Rose fussed with her nails, determined not to get drawn into the daytime TV show on the huge plasma screen. She needed to worry. To think. God, she was so not looking forward to this. But something was obscuring her vision, couldn't be ignored any longer, and with a high flying career in the media, she had to get it fixed fast or she'd lose her job.

This guy offered a fabulous inner city clinic, quick service and reasonable fees. Lunchtime treatments, in fact. Even Botox. She might have some of that too.

"Doctor is ready for you now, Ms Rose," said the smoothly coiffed receptionist with the lovely green eyes.

Wow - what a great looking guy! Lovely dancing blue eyes that appraised her appreciatively with one swift, well-practised glance. And a pretty, dark haired assistant with the most amazing green eyes. Like brilliant emeralds glinting in the light. Had to be contacts...

Scarlett lay back in Dr Coldman's leather chair and stared up at the ceiling as instructed.

"Nothing to worry about, Poppet," said the twinkly doctor. "Just going to pop in some drops - a little anaesthetic, okay?"

She nodded.

"Now what's your favourite movie? Talk to me."

She tried to. Had that been a little jab in her arm while she was concentrating on the doctor? Something. But suddenly she couldn't move. Not a muscle. Nothing. Paralysed by fear? Did that really happen?

Her eyes widened and widened. A pair of vivid green ones loomed over her. Those contacts.

A disembodied female voice. "She'll feel it for sure. Oh God - I need to feed." The sound of deep inhalations. "Feel the pain....the energy...Gouge them out. Gouge them out, Max..."

Just before she passed out, Scarlett saw the implement - a metal hook with a serrated edge - and heard the laughter...

24
THE WITCHFINDERS

Beth clasped her cloak around her. The last day of October and the air was damp and chill, the death of Autumn leaves lying ankle deep in the woods, smoke curling into the night air from her distant cottage. Not far to go now. She bent her head, fear knotting her stomach, knowing what she had yet to pass on the lane.

The party in town had turned riotous. What had at first been ghoulish fancy dress, cut-out gourds and innocent apple-bobbing, had quickly escalated into fighting when the witch finders arrived. 1645 was a dangerous year for young girls not married, and two selling corn dollies had just been dragged away from the market place. Reputedly, and from a reliable source, said the witch finders, they had the devil's marks on them. One had a mole on her neck and the other had been seen conversing with a 'familiar' - a large black dog - in the fields near her cottage. The crowd had gasped, closing in around the girls as they were led away screaming their innocence.

Who would tell such tales about young girls to the merciless witch finders? They surely knew the fate that would await them? Scores of young women in these Eastern counties had been burned to death in less than a year. If you didn't bleed you were a witch, they said. If you had renounced baptism then the water would reject you and a witch would float. If you hadn't then you would drown.

Amid the masks and the smoke, witches costumes and beer-swilling, Beth made a quiet escape, leaving her father and brother behind with the pony and trap. *Not far to go. Not far to go.* Breathlessly she emerged from the short cut through the woods and onto the lane that led to the family home. Just the spooky scarecrow to pass. The one that stood alone in the long-since harvested fields with its leery grin and gangly, flapping limbs. Why couldn't their farming neighbours take it down? Instead they left it there for screeching crows to perch on, in their ragged coats of black cloth. And that monster's head to twist and turn as she hurried past.

She broke into a run. *Don't look at it. Don't look at it. It isn't alive - it's just straw and old clothes...*

The October mist had settled on the lowlands like a blanket of soft grey down, thickening the night air. It was hard to see more than a few footsteps ahead and the light from her lantern glowed a woolly yellow. She kept her eyes fixed on the cottage lights ahead, gritting her teeth and stumbling on towards the glow of a fire in the downstairs room, and a lamp left burning in her bedroom window.

After all - it was Halloween and only fools left themselves and their homes unprotected. By midnight Samhain would begin - two days during which the lining between the living and the dead overlapped and the dead came to life. The only way to protect yourself was to wear masks and costumes, light bonfires and hang lanterns. Confusion was all. By midnight a young girl must be home.

It was a huge relief to push open the cottage door and bolt it behind her. Something about that scarecrow. Her father said she was being ridiculous - that her imagination was wildly out of control. He'd painstakingly shown her how to make her own scarecrow for their small vegetable plot. And yet...just something about that one on the lane...

It haunted her, of course, haunting her dreams as she dozed in front of the fire with the cat purring contentedly on her lap - arms of straw scratching at the windows and slashed out eyes peering in. *Someone there*! She woke with a start,, immediately alert. The cat was meowing, pawing at the door. Something was outside - it hadn't been a dream. She strained her ears. Dull, scraping footsteps. Coming nearer. It was almost midnight. The scarecrow - of course - the scarecrow had come to life just like she always knew it would.

Beth's heart banged against her ribs as with shaking hands she picked up her father's heavy musket. Midnight chimed. Samhain had begun. Her poor father and brother would be coming home, dull witted with drink, relying on the old pony to trot along the familiar route. The monster would surely kill them.

Trembling, she leaned against the barred door, listening to heavy, laboured breathing like an old man with a bad chest - getting louder - footsteps that sounded like a lame man dragging one leg, a smell of wet straw and rotting leaves. She waited, expecting the lightest of taps, or a toothless dead-eyed face staring through the window.

Instead the door was s pounded with iron fists making it rattle on its hinges and she flew backwards. That bolt, she knew, would not hold for long. Over and over the unseen force pummelled and kicked until at last the door splintered and there seemed no choice but to lift the heavy musket and fire. *Be gone horrible scarecrow. Be gone!*

In the silent seconds that followed Beth picked up her lantern and found, to her amazement, not a scarecrow lying on the ground but two grown men. The witch finders. Sent, she realised, to arrest her - a thirteen year old girl. One of the men groaned and she reached for the iron kettle, fire hot, and swung it clean against his skull.

To think that all this time she'd been frightened of a stupid scarecrow, firing blindly at what she thought was a bundle of sticks come to life! But who had sent them out here? It seemed there were people in this town who had called in the witch finders and chosen for her a sure death. How could they do that? Well they had better start praying because she would hunt them down and make them pay. One way. Or another.

***

From the fields opposite the scarecrow swayed and drooped from his post in the darkness. The young girl in the cottage had her hands raised and her face held up to the night sky as she chanted. A few stars glittered between the parting clouds. Samhain. A time for the dead to arise, although he was sorely weakened in his guise as a scarecrow. He'd done what he had to, to warn her they were coming - put her on her guard, scratching at her door and windows to wake her. A girl with a cat. A girl who cast magic circles, stuck pins in effigies and made herbal potions. A witch who would now wreak revenge.

Good, he thought with a dry chuckle. Confusion reigned - let Halloween commence.

25
HOUSE HUNT

So far it had been a disaster. Josie sat, arms folded, staring at the scenery whizzing past: another petrol station, another row of houses…her interest long gone. Nothing they saw now could possibly pick up her mood.

The day had started badly. The first house, after a long drive to the South coast, had been deserted. No one home. No key. No estate agent. Nothing. Tired and tetchy, Josie and Phil stared at each other in disbelief.

"You must have got the wrong day," Phil said.

Josie scrabbled for her diary, and pointed to the correct date and time quite clearly written after confirming with the agents the day before. She'd wanted to scream, really badly, but by then a kindly neighbour had appeared and she'd had to put on a brave face.

The next house had been a gorgeous old cottage with wisteria clambering up the yellow stone walls. Her spirits had lifted. Momentarily. The ceiling beams were so low Phil could barely straighten up, and the staircase so narrow they'd had to scuttle up like mice. That was when she knew it was going to be one of those days.

"This isn't looking good either," she muttered, as Phil turned onto a long, straight windswept road.

"Does look a bit bleak,' Phil admitted. Poor Phil; they'd been house-hunting for weeks now and he was due to start his new job next month. They really did have to find somewhere.

Then the road began to bend and wind and they saw on the left a small copse and a lychgate. "Aha!" Phil brightened. "This must be it!" It certainly looked like the photograph on the brochure: a stone church nestling in a cluster of evergreens.

"I like it," he said, as they walked up to the huge oak door. He pulled on the rope and a large iron bell clanged dramatically. "Wow!"

Josie smiled nervously. "Why do I suddenly feel like I'm in a Hitchcock film?" she asked, just as the door swung open.

The church had been converted just a few years previously and the dining room, photographed to spectacular effect in the brochure, did not disappoint. A long table had been stage set with full dinner service and wine goblets.

"Wow!" said Phil, again

The owner beamed proudly. "And these," he said, pointing to stones set in the walls, "are memorial tablets. This one's dated 1485. Now, shall I organise some tea while you both have a wander?"

Josie looked through an archway to a dark, windowless cavern where a woman and a young girl were baking cakes. "Lovely. Thank you."

"Come on," said Phil. "Let's go look upstairs."

Phil was grinning, Josie noted with some degree of alarm. He loved it. In fact she reckoned he'd already made up his mind, but it was she who would be spending time alone here, and for an illustrator the place was dark.

She ducked to enter the main bedroom. "I bet it's

haunted," she whispered.

Phil squeezed her hand. "Yeah - great, isn't it?"

Downstairs they found a log fire crackling invitingly, and the woman they'd seen earlier was curled up on the sofa with a child.

"Hi, I'm Ellie," said the woman. "And this is Flora, my daughter."

"Josie. Hi." They shook hands.

"Your husband seems very taken with the place?"

"Yes."

Phil was talking to the man they now knew as Alex, admiring the garden. Or more accurately - graveyard.

They had to get out of here. Josie took a welcome sip of hot tea. "Have you had much interest?"

Ellie laughed. "Oh they're all frightened out of their wits. It's the gravestones - not everyone can live in a church."

Josie swallowed another gulp of tea, plucking up courage to ask the next question. She feigned a light, carefree laugh. "Frightened? Er...of ghosts you mean?"

Immediately Flora grinned wickedly and looked set to open her mouth when Ellie quickly interjected, "We don't have ghosts," she said firmly. But Josie noticed her grip on Flora's shoulder tighten, and Flora had begun to look annoyed and kick her heels against the sofa.

"I know," Ellie said. "Let's show them the garden, Alex."

A bank of black cloud, edging closer, was casting a dark shadow over the church, whipping up a sharp breeze. And reluctant to move from the warm fire after a long, tiring day, Josie stayed pinned to her seat. "I think I'll stay here if you don't mind?"

"Sure. Flora will keep you company."

Good. If there was one thing she knew about kids - they told it like it was. "So," she said to Flora once they were alone. "How do you feel about having gravestones in the garden? It must be spooky sometimes?"

"They're not harmful, you know," said Flora, with an air of authority. Then more sheepishly, "Granny says we do have ghosts though, and she won't come to stay with us anymore."

"Really?"

"She said someone was trying to pull the bedclothes off her bed all night."

Eek! "Has that ever happened to you?"

Flora shook her head. "No. Apart from Arthur. But he's a friendly ghost."

"Uh-huh." Yup. They definitely had to get out of here.

The black cloud was now directly overhead and it wasn't long before the others practically blew back in through the French windows, the doors slamming shut behind them.

"We'll definitely be in touch," Phil said, handing Alex his business card. "We absolutely love it, don't we, darling?"

Josie nodded and smiled. Over her dead body!

"Apart from the fact that it's dark and haunted, it's totally isolated," she argued as they drove away. "Look!" Sure enough, as soon as they turned out of the driveway, the landscape was bleak and barren again. Around them the wind howled.

"We need to turn round," said Phil, glancing at the time. There was still another house to see.

"How long to get there?"

"About half an hour. Ah - here we go." He swung the car into a narrow lane flanked by swaying trees. And then stopped dead. In front of them was an entire village: a row of stone cottages, a stream, a manor house and a church. "This is it," Phil cried excitedly. "Alex said the whole area was an ancient Saxon settlement. Blimey - look at it."

Josie, with her artist's eye, noticed the eerie, low golden light and the wild, dark sky skirting around it. There wasn't a soul in sight. But Phil was now in raptures about the fascinating history and buying a metal detector for ancient treasures.   Eventually, noticing her silence he glanced over and patted her hand. "You're not seriously spooked are you?"

Josie nodded. "I can't live here." And then felt rotten because he looked so crestfallen. "Let's just see what the next house is like before we decide, okay?"

"You don't seem to like anything," he grumbled.

That was unfair and he knew it. The move from North to South was a huge task and so far they'd seen cottages Phil couldn't stand up in, and houses either on busy junctions or needing total renovation, when neither of them were any good at DIY. All of which made the church appeal so much to Phil. It had character, he argued. It had space. It had history. Peace and quiet...

Josie bit her lip. Time was running out.

Half an hour later they pulled up outside a perfectly normal brick house on the outskirts of a working village. There was a pub, a post office, and even a tiny village school. Josie smiled. Normality. Why had it been so hard to find?

A pleasant looking lady in her late fifties, opened the door, wiping her hands on her apron. "Madeline Oliver," she said, offering her hand. "Come on in. You must be exhausted travelling all the way from Yorkshire? I'll put the kettle on while you have a look round."

The house was large, light and airy. The garden swept down to a delightful stream and there was even an outhouse that could be used as a studio.

"It's perfect," Josie beamed.

Phil shrugged.

"Oh come on," she urged as they strolled hand in hand around the garden. "I can live here when you're away without being scared to death. There are neighbours, a shop and a community. Even a studio. Look Phil, we're not going to get any better than this and it's a good price too."

Phil looked around and eventually nodded. "Well I liked the church but, well, you need to be safe and…"

Josie leaned into him and squeezed his arm.

Ten minutes later they were getting back into the car amid promises of phoning the agent first thing. The light was fading fast and they had a long journey home but finally, finally - the search was over.

***

Madeline Oliver watched as their taillights disappeared round the corner, then looked at her watch. She mustn't be late. Tonight was Vernal Equinox, and as High Priestess she must cast the circle for the Wicca ceremony before dark. The whole village would be there. And there was news - they had newcomers to look forward to welcoming soon. Very soon.

ABOUT THE AUTHOR

Sarah England originally trained as a nurse in Sheffield, before spending 20 years in pharmaceutical sales - specialising in mental health. She has now been writing fiction for around 8 years, with over 140 short stories published to date; in national magazines such as Woman's Weekly, My Weekly and Take a Break, plus various newspapers, like The Sunday Telegraph and The Weekly News. Overseas publications include That's Life and Woman's Day in Australia, and You in South Africa. She has also had a 3 part murder-mystery serial published by Woman's Weekly (March 2013), and has several anthology inclusions, notably with Bridge House Publishers, and most recently Alfie Dog, with whom she has several light comedies and spoof fairy stories. With a preference for comedy and horror, her humorous novel, Expected, will be published June '13, and she is currently working on a supernatural thriller. Writing fiction, to entertain and amuse, is all she has ever wanted to do, and she hopes to continue long into her dotage. Sarah lives in Dorset with her husband, Don, and spaniel, Harry.
http://www.sarahengland.yolasite.com

Printed in Great Britain
by Amazon.co.uk, Ltd.,
Marston Gate.